Muppit Boy and the Allergies of Evil

Adventures of Muppit Boy
Book 1

Michael J. Bowler

Muppit Boy and the Allergies of Evil

First Edition: 2026

Paperback ISBN: 979-8-9936486-0-6

Hardback ISBN: 979-8-9936486-1-3

eBook ISBN: 979-8-9936486-2-0

Editor: Loretta Sylvestre

Cover Art: Pintado

Chapter Heading Illustrations: Hanna Boanna

For my son who,
at age eleven,
read this book all the way through
without my prompting
(a rare occurrence)
and gave it his stamp of approval.
Love you, son!

Contents

Chapter 1

What Was That?

"Hey, look, it's Muppit Boy and his crew!"

I freeze across the street from St. Mary's parking lot, which is currently barricaded by police cars. Kids and parents mill around on the sidewalk craning their necks for a looksee at whatever's going on at my school. I'm dying to know, too, but first things first.

I turn toward the source of those words, even though I already know who shouted them: beefy bully Mason Rizzo. He's flanked, as usual, by his two partners in crime, athletic Lorenzo Mazza and dumb-as-a-rock Julian Briggs.

Kash steps up beside me and I feel her whole body stiffen with anger.

"Uh, Kash." My best friend, Barney, slips an empty candy wrapper into his pocket and gives his lips a quick swipe with one chubby hand. "There's too many people around."

Kash is coiled, like a cheetah about to spring at its next meal.

"He's right, Kash," I say, worried that she might ignore me. "And Rizzo is only talking smack 'cause he's across the street and there're cops around."

Kashvi Jindal is a pretty Indian girl with long, black hair who's so seriously into martial arts that *boys* are scared of her! Even Rizzo. Since Kash joined up with Barn and me this year as part of our little detective agency—she wants to be a forensics specialist when she grows up—Rizzo hasn't punked us once, except from a distance.

We make an odd threesome. Kash is tall and lean. I'm shorter than short. And Barn is big and round. When we walk down the street side by side we look like we're spelling the word "Oil." I'm the "i," obviously.

I decide to distract Rizzo, if that's possible with a kid so dense. "What's going on at school?"

We're only a side street apart from each other, but Rizzo's normal voice is foghorn loud. "Somebody broke in. Trashed some of the rooms. Is the Muppit Boy detective agency going to investigate?" He laughs, which sounds like water gurgling down a drain.

I'm considering how to respond to his taunt when Barn pipes up in his own bullhorn fashion, "Hey, we're good detectives. We found the principal's cell phone when it went missing last month."

The gurgling laugh erupts again. "Yeah, that was a real

Sherlock moment for you losers. I could have figured out he left it in the bathroom."

"Yeah, but you didn't," Kash calls out, her tone piercing and clipped, "because detective work requires intelligence, something you lack. Oh, and I'm sure you remember how *we* uncovered the thief who stole that field trip money from Sister Anna's class? As I recall, your friend, the thief, got expelled. How sad." A taunting grin spreads across her face.

Rizzo loses his smirk and squints with feral anger, which is something to behold because of his enormous eyebrows. I mean, they're *caterpillar* big, especially for a twelve-year-old, and when he squints they turn into a unibrow so massive it looks like a snake.

I fix my attention on the activity in the parking lot. Cops move back and forth from the front entrance of the two-story school building and the entire parking lot is cordoned off with yellow "Police Line: Do Not Cross" tape. Among the uniformed officers, I spot my Big Brother, Ari, in his grey suit and blue tie. Since making detective, Ari always sports suits that make him look like a businessman. I'd love to run over and get his attention, but he's clearly busy. If there's one thing I've learned from my Mom posting videos of my most humiliating moments on her YouTube channel, it's how *not* to embarrass someone in front of their peers.

I return my focus to Rizzo. "Who knows, Rizzo, one day I might be the detective who busts you for hiding stolen goods in your eyebrows."

Barn cracks up and Kash chuckles with delight. But the best part is how Mazza and Briggs bust up and Rizzo's face flames so red I can see it from where I'm standing. He balls up his thick fists like he might rush across the street and throw a punch.

"One of these days, Muppit Boy, you won't have Wonder Woman around for protection," he booms loud enough for other kids to turn away from the action at school and look our way. "And when that happens, I'm gonna make that giant nose of yours even bigger!"

Another nose joke. Between that and the infamous Muppit Boy videos all over the internet, is there any wonder my self-esteem is in the toilet? I shake off these thoughts and glance around for an escape route. This street runs alongside St. Mary's and there's a wall and alley separating the rear of the school from the houses behind it. My detective brain is thinking that if *I* broke into the school, for whatever reason, I'd probably sneak out the back, or likely even break in *through* the back. There may be clues to find and if the cops are focused on searching inside the school, we might have a few minutes to look.

"Hey, Mo, you should march right up to Rizzo and use that trick pen Kash gave you," Barn says, leaning across Kash and lowering his voice. "I wanna see how it works."

I feel the pen in my pocket. Kash says it will work great against Rizzo and wants me to have it for occasions, like, well, that time I was in the boys' bathroom and Rizzo used toilet paper to tie me up like a mummy while his sidekicks held me down. I managed to rip my way out pretty easily, but they filmed me first—especially my nose sticking out of the paper—and shared the vid around school. Kash was furious that I didn't report the incident, but being a snitch would've only made things worse.

In any case, I've already forgotten Rizzo because I *really* want to scope out the back of St. Mary's. When the Sherlock thing meets my ADHD, resistance is futile.

"I think we should creep around back and check that alley for clues, in case the perp went in or out that way."

"Cool," Barn says so loudly that Rizzo takes a step back, like he thinks we're going to rush him. "Can I use the magnifying glass this time?"

"Sure." I turn to Kash, but she's seriously giving Rizzo the evil eye. "Kash?"

"Yeah, I'm down," she replies, almost as though she isn't listening to me. "But first we teach Eyebrow Boy a lesson."

Before I can respond, she's marching across the street. True to form, Mazza and Briggs turn tail and run into the crowd, but Rizzo just freezes.

Not knowing what Kash will do, I follow and Barn waddles after me.

Completely fearless, Kash stops right in front of Rizzo, despite him being thicker and taller. Rizzo takes a step back and raises his fists. I stop at Kash's side, and Barn huffs and puffs his way to mine.

"Kash," I mutter, "he's not worth getting suspended for."

"Muppit Boy's right, Wonder Woman," Rizzo says, trying hard to sound brave, but I detect the quaver in his voice. "And I don't like hitting girls."

"Like you could land a punch on me?" Kash laughs—it's a dangerous laugh. She clearly wants to go all Bruce Lee on him here and now. "Go back under the rock you crawled out from, Rizzo, and leave my friends alone. Or else."

She glowers and he flinches back. Then Kash whips her head around so hard her fishtail braid slaps Rizzo in the face with a sharp *thwack* sound. Barn gasps with surprise, as does the small group of kids surrounding us. Rizzo cries out in shock as Kash struts away down the side street toward the rear of St. Mary's. Barn eyes me for a split second before loping after her.

I note the stunned look on Rizzo's face and the red mark blooming on his cheek. I can't help but smile as I hurry after my friends. He doesn't even shout out any hollow threats.

We reach the alley and creep around the backside of the school, eyeing the dumpsters resting against the faded brick building. I wave the others up against the building so I can peer around the corner without being seen.

Two uniformed officers stand guard on the opposite side of the dumpsters, no doubt watching the rear door into the cafeteria. I recognize them from Ari's precinct, and I don't want them to see me. In any case, everything back here seems quiet. As soon as the officers turn away from my direction, I motion to the others, and we dart across the mouth of the alley to duck behind a stone wall separating the front yard of a two-story house from the back of the school.

Of course, Barn just *has* to trip over his shoelaces—*again* —and tumble to the sidewalk with a loud grunt of pain. I whip a finger to my lips with a "Shush!" while Kash scowls something fierce. Barn's round face glows red with embarrassment, giving him an unsettling similarity to a pig, especially with his small, upturned nose and red hair. He fumbles with the laces while Kash rises onto her tiptoes to peer over the wall.

"What do you see?" I keep my voice to a whisper, despite all the chatter and police radio sounds wafting over from the front of the school.

"There's a jagged hole in the school wall on our side of the dumpsters."

"How big?"

"'Bout the size of a grapefruit, I'd say. The bricks are broken, like something pushed its way out." She looks over the wall again for a few seconds and then down at me. "And there's something shiny leading away from the hole."

Perplexed, I turn to Barn for his take. He has his shoelaces tangled up into knots and uses fingers that look like small sausages to try and untangle them. Barney and shoelaces have *never* been friends, but his mom won't let him wear loafers to school.

I swallow my pride. "Uh, Kash, could you, uh, give me a boost up?"

I know my face is redder than a bottle of ketchup, but I maintain eye contact with Kash. Being the smallest twelve-year-old boy on the planet pretty much means swallowing your pride daily.

Kash drops low, linking the fingers of both hands together into a step for my foot.

I check the bottom of my shoe to make sure there's no dog poop or gum and then plant it squarely within her cupped hands. With more strength than you'd expect from a girl who's so slim, she presses me upward and I grip the top of the wall.

The cops aren't looking my way—phew!—so I check out the hole she described. It's jagged, the edges rough, like something plowed through at high speed. It doesn't look like someone cut through the wall with a tool or drill.

I scan the ground, squinting against the morning sun, and follow the barely visible trail leading away from the hole. It crosses the asphalt of the alley to a Folger's coffee can lying on the ground below me. Maybe the can was tossed over the fence from the backyard of this house or maybe it fell out of the school dumpster. But no matter how it got there, it's currently moving.

I gasp and hear, "What's wrong?" from Kash below me, but I don't look away from the moving can. It acts like something inside is trying to get out. I hold my breath. The can completes a full turn.

Something dark and thick—like a living cigar—oozes its way out into the sunlight. It's a slug! An enormous slug! And it almost acts like it sees me.

"Hey, you kids!" One of the officers sprints past the dumpsters.

That's when the slug lunges forward, straight at the wall as fast as a dog!

I jump from Kash's hand bridge to the sidewalk.

"What—"

I push Kash to one side and then shove Barn in the other direction before diving after him.

I'm just in time.

The rocks of the wall blow outward in a shattering hailstorm of chunks and shards of masonry. As I land hard on one shoulder, my glasses slip, but I catch a glimpse of the slug zipping down the side street away from St. Mary's at very high speed!

Screeching tires assail my ears and a plain black sedan sails past in pursuit. I barely catch a sideways peek of the passenger as he peers out the window. He wears dark shades and a dark suit. Then he's gone. The car careens around the next corner and vanishes.

"Mo!"

My Big Brother pelts along the sidewalk toward me, followed by a boatload of cops and many of my peers. My hands are scraped from slamming into the pavement, and I struggle to get my bearings as I rise to my knees and slide my glasses back up my nose.

"What was that?" Kash is still on the ground, brushing herself off and glaring at me, ignoring the crowd bearing down on us. "A bomb?"

I'm too shaken to respond. Barn grips one knee, grimacing in pain. It's obvious he didn't see anything either. As the pounding footsteps grow closer, I manage a quick glance at the stone wall. The lower portion sports a large hole of blasted rock that's easily the size of a small soccer ball. Bits of colored stone lay strewn about the sidewalk and some shards even landed in my hair.

Did I see what I thought I saw?

"Mo, are you all right?" Ari's strong hands grip me under my arms and pull me up.

I gaze into his worried face and want to hug him, but I spot Rizzo and the other kids, and I refuse to look weak in front of them. I step clear of Ari so he—and the kids—will see me standing on my own.

One officer helps Barn to his feet, but a glare from Kash sends another cop back a step, and then she stands without assistance.

Many kids in the crowd are filming me with their phones. Rizzo smirks with glee, but my science teacher offers me a smile of encouragement.

Officers examine the hole in the wall. A faint, shiny trail leads away from it and down the street.

"Mo."

I turn back to Ari. He's a big man, six feet four, to be exact, and I feel like a hobbit whenever I'm with him. But he's never once made me feel like a hobbit or anything less than the most important person in his life.

"I'm okay, Ari," I finally say because he's checking me for injuries.

"What happened? What did that?" He points to the hole in the wall.

I brush some stone chips from my thick black hair. "A slug."

There's this long moment of *really* heavy silence. Seriously, it's so quiet I think I can hear boats down at the harbor, and that's blocks away. Then I hear laughter, and eye the kids from St. Mary's. They're laughing.

"Excuse me?"

Ari's tone is one of disbelief. I've helped him investigate some strange cases over the years—like a cat burglar who stole real cats—but nothing like what I just saw.

"It was a huge slug, Ari. Like this." I spread my hands about six inches apart. "It blasted through the wall and took off that way." I point down the empty street.

Ari stares at me with his mouth hanging open, and the laughter of my peers increases. The teachers tell the kids to be quiet, but, if anything, the hilarity increases.

Detective Carter, Ari's unkempt partner, chews gum and squints at me like I'm being my usual smart-aleck self.

I give him a steely look. "Seriously, I'm telling the truth."

He grunts and fixes his beady brown eyes onto Barn. "You see a slug?"

Barn is red-faced and flustered, still fiddling with his tangled laces. "No, I was trying to get this knot out of my laces."

More laughter fills the air, accompanied by more admonishments from St. Mary's teachers.

Carter shifts his gaze toward Kash. "You?"

"No. Mo pushed me out of the way. I just heard the wall explode and saw that black car go by."

"A guy in that car looked right at me," I tell Ari, desperate to be validated.

Ari's tight facial expression eases, like having a human suspect to pursue is better than, well, a slug. "What did he look like?"

My mind rewinds the scene. That's the only way to describe what I can do. My brain records everything like a video camera and I can "play back" the footage as needed. I "watch" the black car speed past me and focus on the guy in the passenger seat.

"Short black hair, dark suit, Caucasian, dark sunglasses."

A voice that's unmistakably Rizzo's calls out, "First a super slug and now the Men in Black. Muppit Boy strikes again!"

The kids howl with merriment, and I burn so red they should call me Lobster Boy and throw me into a pot of boiling water to put me out of my misery. I can't even meet Ari's gaze because I'm so embarrassed. I feel a large hand on my shoulder and look up at my Big Brother.

"I'll take you home and we can talk about it there." Ari turns to Carter. "Interview Barn and Kash and anyone else, especially about that black car. That's one tangible piece of evidence we all saw."

Carter grunts, pulling out his little notebook and turning to face my friends.

"C'mon, Mo." Ari starts leading me toward the front of the school.

"We'll be over later," Kash calls after me.

I can't help but smile when Barn pipes up with, "We will?" and Kash lets out a loud, exasperated sigh.

I don't even glance at the grinning, mocking faces of my peers, but just stare at the sidewalk as Ari leads me past the crowd. He's big and a cop, so even Rizzo doesn't say anything nasty.

But I hear him chuckle.

Chapter 2

I Wonder What Slug Dump Feels Like When It Hits You

Mom engulfs me in a crushing hug the moment Ari and me walk into the house because, well, kids streamed me live—post-slug attack—sounding like a fool, and she'd watched it all.

"Elmo Fitzroy, what were you thinking, sneaking around the back of the school like that?" she begins, her voice rising in pitch like it always does when she's exasperated with me—which is, like, every day. "You could've been killed!"

I pull away from her suffocating mass of bushy hair and glower. I'm not really mad at her, more upset that I might have disappointed Ari.

"You could have gotten another million followers, Mom. The death of Muppit Boy. Your biggest show yet."

She rears back in horror, like she can't believe I just said what I said. I can't either.

"Elmo!" Her face twists into a mask of horror.

I glance sheepishly at Ari. He doesn't need to say anything. I see the disapproval in his squinting eyes. "I'm sorry, Mom, that was mean. I'm just rattled. You know how that messes with my ADHD."

She eyes me in that way she sometimes does that makes me squirm. I imagine her thinking how she wishes I wasn't her son. I guess I would drive me crazy, too, if I had a kid like me.

"I know how you feel about the whole Muppit Boy thing, and I've apologized a *thousand* times. But that was cruel, what you just said."

I grow hot with shame. My mom excels in the laying-on-of-guilt department, but in this case, she's right.

"I'm sorry."

I step forward and hug her tightly. She flinches a moment, maybe because I haven't voluntarily hugged her in, like, forever. Then she wraps her arms around me, and we stand in that embarrassing posture for a few moments.

By way of explaining, Mom has this super-popular YouTube channel about being a single parent and I've been her star attraction since birth. Here's the problem. First off, my name is Elmo. Secondly, Mom always dressed me in this furry red onesie so I looked like a certain famous puppet. Third, I have a big nose. A *really* big nose. And I've always worn big glasses that made my nose look even bigger—kind of like the front end of an Air Force jet. I stopped looking at the comments on Mom's channel years ago because they were pretty nasty. But, thanks to those comments about my, well, larger-than-normal facial feature, and the red onesie, I became known the world over—and *especially* here in San Pedro—as "Muppit Boy."

Ari clears his throat and that's my excuse to pull away without Mom getting mad.

"I need to talk with Mo, Abigail, about what happened, take an official statement. Do I have your permission?"

She gazes at him in amazement, like she can't believe he felt the need to ask after all his years being part of our family.

"Of course, Aristotle."

She always calls Ari by his full name. I admit, it's cool. Ari's parents came over here from Greece and that's how he got the name.

"Best use his room downstairs because I'm getting so much chatter online about what happened. I need to respond."

My stomach twists into knots. "Is everybody laughing at me, like always?"

"No, honey," Mom says, but doesn't meet my gaze.

"C'mon, Mo." Ari places a hand on my shoulder and offers a reassuring smile.

I turn slowly toward the stairs leading down to my basement room. Ari follows.

Ari's been my Big Brother since I was seven and he's the only "dad" I've ever known because mine died of cancer before I was even two. The Big Brothers Big Sisters program matches up boys with no father in the home to a mentor who sees him on weekends, so the boy can have a male role model. From the moment Ari walked into my house—tall, confident, and built—my seven-year-old heart was captured. Back then, my ADHD was all over the map and so was I. I drove Ari crazy on every outing, but he never lost his cool. I would get mad about my mom, or being called Muppit Boy, or school, or even the food we were eating, and I'd lose it. But he'd just let me get my anger out and then we would go do something fun.

Later, when we'd be at an arcade or playing mini-golf and I'd calmed down, he'd talk with me about how men need to direct their anger in ways that won't hurt other people. He told me tons of stories about how, when he was a kid, he used to throw furniture at people who made him mad. He wanted to be a cop all his life and when he was thirteen an officer told him at a school career day that self-control was a job requirement. So, Ari learned to master his anger, and he's taught me self-control, too, mostly by modeling it. He's also helped guide my hyper brain toward detective skills by allowing me to assist with a few of his cases. For a guy who's never had kids of his own, Ari's been everything I could've wanted in a Big Brother, and so much more. With my mom turning me into an international freak show, trust me, I *needed* Ari.

That's why, as we go downstairs to my room, I feel like

somebody punched me in the stomach and knocked all the air from my lungs because I'm convinced he doesn't believe me.

"So, tell me exactly what you saw," Ari says once we're seated in front of my desk, and he has his pad and pen at the ready.

I pause a moment to calm down, eyeing some of my rocket and superhero models dangling from the ceiling. Having always wanted to fly, I've obsessed over every flying thing there is since I can remember. When my heartbeat finally slows to a normal rhythm, I "rewind" my brain and review "footage" of what I saw when Kash hefted me up to look over the wall. I describe everything that happened in great detail, while Ari says nothing—just takes notes. He knows how my brain works and how I need to finish the description at my own pace. I finally "see" no more details I think are important and fall silent.

I study Ari as he finishes scribbling in his little notebook and the only sound in the room is that pen scratching at the paper. He strokes his small, well-trimmed beard as he writes.

"Do you believe me, Ari?"

He seems momentarily surprised. Then his face shifts and I guess he realizes what I'm thinking. "Of course, I do, Mo. I did back at school, too, but it just sounded so crazy."

I sag with relief. "I know. But it happened."

He sticks the back of the pen into his mouth like a straw and considers a moment. Then he removes it. "Car. Did you get the plate number?"

I replay the footage of the car careening past me down the street. While I wasn't conscious at the time of the license plate, now I make it out with clarity.

"It says 'U.S. Government' at the top. On the left is 'DHS' in capital letters followed by the numbers 21354. Then it says, 'For Official Use Only' at the bottom."

Ari grins as he writes it down. "Wish I had that video recorder brain of yours."

"And my ADHD?"

"Well, not that." He holds out a fist and we bump.

My brain tends to shift gears on a dime and my mood shifts with it. I slump again and he scoots his chair closer.

"What's wrong?"

"You heard my mom," I say solemnly. "Just when I thought it was safe *not* to be Muppit Boy anymore, everyone thinks I'm crazy on top of being a loser."

"You know I don't like you calling yourself a loser." His voice is as stern as it ever gets with me.

I look down and shrug. "It's true."

He reaches out and tilts my chin up with one hand so I can meet his gaze straight on. "Mo, who's my boy?"

"Me."

"What else did I tell you that first day we met?"

I don't need to rewind that moment in my brain. It will be forever glued to my heart. "We're a team."

"Both of those are forever true."

I see the love in his eyes and almost tear up, but I've

already been dweeby enough today, so I just nod. "Thanks, Ari."

He pulls his hand back and eyes me a long moment. "Anything else you can think of that might be relevant?"

I have good instincts, so I pause and consider everything that's been happening the past few days and a gut feeling arises from deep within me.

"I think it's all connected."

He tilts his head quizzically. "What is?"

"The super slug and the hearing aid thief you're hunting."

Some old lady in a clown mask has been stealing hearing aids from people by threatening them with a chainsaw!

His eyebrows shoot up so far I think they might launch right off his forehead. "Why do you say that?"

"A hunch. All the people who got their aids snatched live around here, including two nuns over at St. Mary's. Then that slug attacks the school. I don't think that's by accident."

He breaks into a huge smile. "That's my boy in action. Good analysis!"

He offers a high five and I slap it hard, feeling good about myself for the first time today.

He stands and tucks the notebook into his impeccably neat jacket. I swear he's as neat as I am messy, and I'm *super* messy. But he didn't even comment when he had to step over a pile of clothes to sit down. He never does.

"I'm going back to the station. See if I can find out why Homeland Security was at St. Mary's."

Now my eyebrows shoot up. "Homeland Security?"

"The DHS on those plates. Stands for Department of Homeland Security."

"Oh, no," I mutter. "And that guy looked right at me."

"Nobody's getting my boy. I got your back." He grins.

I return the grin, and he leaves.

I sit a moment and consider everything that's happened.

Heavy feet clomp down the stairs and Barn steps into my room, Kash right behind him. I notice that Barn's shoelaces are properly tied and know, without asking, that Kash undid the knots and fixed them.

They plop down into their usual spots – Barn on top of my double bed and Kash in the chair next to me so she can access the computer.

She tells me that classes have been cancelled until the damage can be assessed and the investigation completed, and I fill them in on everything Ari and I talked about.

Kash eyes me dubiously. "You're sure it was a slug?"

I nod.

Kash is always so mathematical about everything, and obviously a slug blasting through a stone wall doesn't add up.

"If anyone else told me that, I'd laugh."

I confess her words make me feel kind of good inside, but I don't say so.

"Well, I'm just glad the slug missed me," Barn says from the bed.

He pulls a gluten-free chocolate chip granola bar from his pocket and strips off the wrapping. He doesn't have a gluten allergy, but his mom thinks gluten is why Barn is so chubby. I've been to her house for dinner and the problem *isn't* gluten. She serves enough food to feed my entire school, and he eats *all* of it.

Kash squints with annoyance. "Barn, a slug can't hurt you. At least, not a regular one, anyway."

He's about to take a bite from the granola bar. "What if it dumps on me?"

"Huh?" I'm not sure my mile-a-minute brain heard correctly.

"I wonder what slug dump feels like when it hits you," Barn muses thoughtfully as he bites into the bar like a shark ripping flesh off a marlin.

Kash looks at me and rolls her eyes.

"Uh, I don't think that's gonna be a problem, Barn," I offer, trying to keep from laughing.

"Do you think slug dump is as nasty as bird poop?" Barn stops chewing to look at both of us with raised eyebrows.

Kash lifts an angry fist and points it at him. "Do you think this fist is stronger than your face?"

He swallows his mouthful and leans back in fear.

I sigh inside. "Listen, guys, since we have the day off, let's do some detective work."

Kash leans forward in her chair to study me. "Like what?"

"Remember those security cam photos of the hearing aid thief, how she wears those orthopedic old lady shoes?"

"So?" Kash eyes me quizzically.

"So, I found the only store in Pedro that sells them. I say we check it out."

"What good will that do?"

I rummage under the pile of papers and candy wrappers on my desk and pull out a photo I printed last night. It's an enlargement of the shoe the clown lady was wearing. I snagged it off a news website.

"We can ask the store clerk if he knows who bought this shoe and get the address of the buyer."

Kash tilts her head, shifting the fish tail braid to one side. "And the clerk is going to just give you the address?"

I shake my head. "All he has to do is look it up to see if the store sold them. Barn will do the rest."

"Huh?"

I look over at Barn, his cheeks puffed out with the last of the granola bar.

He tries to say, "What?" but it comes out "Waa?"

I grin.

Chapter 3

You're Muppit Boy!

We park and secure our bikes to a lamppost in front of a shoe store called Ortho Kicks and start for the entrance. I spot some kids from school heading our way and quickly duck into the store before they see me. Barn stumbles into me as he follows because Kash pushes him.

"Hurry, they're coming," she hisses as she closes the door.

I manage to keep my feet but need to catch Barn to prevent him from going down. He outweighs me by forty pounds, and it feels like a sack of flour hitting my chest. I grunt with pain.

"May I help you children?"

The voice startles me, and I spin around. "Uh, yes, sir."

I glance at Kash, because she's the one to tip off Barn

when the time is right, and she nods. Then I saunter as casually as I can past a series of tall racks laden with shoes of varying shapes and sizes. The only color combinations are variations on white, black, brown, and gray. Nobody under eighty would be caught dead in these "kicks."

The man behind the counter is old. No, *ancient* is a better word. Like maybe he was Thomas Edison's first grade teacher back in the day? Yeah, that old! His face looks like a relief map of the world's great rivers. And the glasses are so thick his eyes are the size of golf balls. Even as I'm thinking these pretty rude thoughts—me, the dork of all dorks—the man smiles, and my stomach tightens with shame.

At least, until he exclaims, "You're Muppit Boy! My wife thinks you're adorable!"

I'm scowling, but he doesn't seem to notice. Guess those Coke bottle lenses need updating.

"Our favorite episode was the one where you were at some petting zoo holding a duck and the duck bit your nose."

He laughs and I'm on fire with embarrassment.

"She's not here now, but *oooh*, my wife would *love* an autograph."

I want to shrink into the floor, like I always do when someone recognizes me from that show. But then I get a brilliant idea and scrap my original plan.

"Sure, sir, I'd be happy to give you an autograph. I have a favor to ask for my mom, anyway."

He fumbles around on the counter for a pen.

I've signed lots of autographs over the years, mostly for mothers or small kids, so I've perfected this really dorky script for writing "Muppit Boy."

I glance back to see Kash and Barn pretending to study some ugly "kicks" on one of the racks, and then I turn to find the old man holding out a purple Sharpie and piece of paper. I adjust my glasses and offer what I hope is a "cute kid" smile.

"How would your wife like a real autographed eight by ten of me?"

His eyes bulge. And yes, my mother *actually* used to send autographed pictures of me to fans for contests she ran.

"She'd love one," the man exclaims, his voice rising with excitement.

I lean in toward the counter, standing on tip toes to make myself seem taller—and so my nose doesn't look like it's resting atop the counter like a paperweight. "Here's the deal, mister...?"

"Loafer," he replies, and I choke back laughter. "Ira. And my wife's name is Penny."

I fight for self-control.

"Well, Mr., uh, Loafer, my mom is putting together a show for people in Pedro who buy your shoes. At least, we think this is one of yours."

I pull the photo from my messenger bag and slide it across the counter like it's some clandestine secret message.

He picks up the photo in one liver spotted hand and then grabs a magnifying glass the size of a tennis racket to examine it.

I wait anxiously.

"Well, yes, indeed, I believe that is one of ours," Loafer says, his voice filled with smug satisfaction. "Perfect for bunions and hammer toes."

I almost lose it again and pretend to be coughing.

"You okay, Muppit Boy?"

I nod but need a moment to compose myself.

He stares at me like I'm a celebrity, which I guess I kind of am.

"My, uh, my mom wants to get in touch with everyone in town who bought those shoes to find out if any of them would like to be on her show."

The old man beams with pride. "Why, that's a swell idea. It might step up our business."

He laughs like he told the best joke ever and I offer my version of a chuckle.

"So, sir, do you keep records of the people who bought this shoe?"

He frowns and his face collapses like an old shirt.

"I suspect so, but my wife is the one who keeps track of everyone. Let me see if I can find sales records in this thing."

That "thing" is a pretty-old-looking desktop computer sitting on the counter about a foot from my face. He starts doing the one-finger typing on a yellowed keyboard and I'm beginning to think I'll still be here for breakfast tomorrow when he exclaims, "Well, what do you know, I found it." He beams, his teeth looking crooked and somewhat yellowed, almost like the keyboard. "I'm rather proud of myself."

I step up even higher onto my tiptoes and once again curse my hobbit size. He reacts by turning the monitor away from me like I have a contagious disease.

"Of course, I can't share personal information with anyone, not even someone as famous as you," he says, sounding almost guilty. "My wife will have to contact these people and have them call your mother. What would her number be, by the way?"

Okay, I guess my "cute kid" look wasn't cute enough, but fortunately Kash and Barn are on the job. I hear a loud clattering, then Barn's voice crying out, and I spin around. My mouth drops open and Mr. Loafer exclaims, "Oh, my word!"

Barn has managed to create a *much* bigger diversion than I asked for. He's still in motion as I turn, tumbling into one of the tall shoe racks. The rack has crashed into the one next to it and then that rack falls against the next one. Like dominoes, the shoe racks tip and fall one after the other, circling the store while Barn sprawls amidst a mountain of shoes and Kash stands like a wax statue with both hands over her mouth.

Even before the final rack topples like a Jenga tower and dumps its contents into a haphazard pile, Mr. Loafer is around the counter flailing his arms and spluttering, "My shoes, my shoes!"

I don't waste a second. I dart behind the counter and examine his computer. There's a list of ten names and addresses on the screen and I whip out my phone. Tapping the camera, I snap several pictures of the screen, then slip the phone back into my pocket and hurry around to help Kash.

Barn is covered in shoes. Seriously, from head to toe. At least three of the closest racks dumped their loads all over him and Kash is digging through them to reach him. Mr. Loafer flaps his arms like he works at the airport flagging down planes, and I feel sorry for him. I told Barn to distract the man, not destroy his store.

Kash and I each find one of Barn's flailing hands and pull. He's like dead weight, but Kash is strong and we manage to extricate him from the mess he created.

I look him up and down. "Are you all right?"

Barn looks sheepish. "Yeah. Never been attacked by ugly shoes before."

I sigh heavily and my stomach lurches with guilt as I look at Mr. Loafer. "He's very sorry, sir. It was an accident."

"But my store!" Loafer whines, almost crying. "My wife will kill me."

My mother will, too, if she finds out. "We'll help put everything back, won't we guys?"

Barn looks at me with surprise. "We will? But I thought you wanted—"

Kash kicks him hard in the shin and he cries out in pain. "We're cleaning this place up. Now." She glares at him, and he doesn't argue.

It takes us over an hour to set the racks back where they were and to more or less get the shoes onto them in something resembling order.

Mr. Loafer flits about like a frustrated bee that's unable to find quite the right flavor of pollen, pointing at this or that rack with exasperation. "No, that one goes over there!"

We do our best, but the irritated man is more than happy to see us leave, especially after Barn knocks over two of the racks we'd just reset. Barn is my best friend, but he puts the "K' in "klutz" any day of the week. Worse than I ever was as a little kid.

Sweating from my exertions, I wave to Mr. Loafer and follow Barn and Kash out of the store. The old man doesn't even ask for my autograph. I guess he's had enough of Muppit Boy.

We unlock our bikes and I turn to Barn. "Next time I ask for a diversion, don't make it so big."

"That wasn't his diversion," Kash mutters with disgust.

"It wasn't?"

I look at Barn and his cheeks become cherry red.

"I, uh, I tripped over my shoelaces and fell into the rack," he admits, his deep-set eyes not meeting my own. "My original plan was just to call the guy over to show me some shoes."

"Bruh." I almost do the face palm but restrain myself.

Kash sighs heavily and shakes her head.

"It's all good. We got what we came for." I hold up my phone and smile. "Time to check out some houses."

Kash grins.

Chapter 4

What Is This Place?

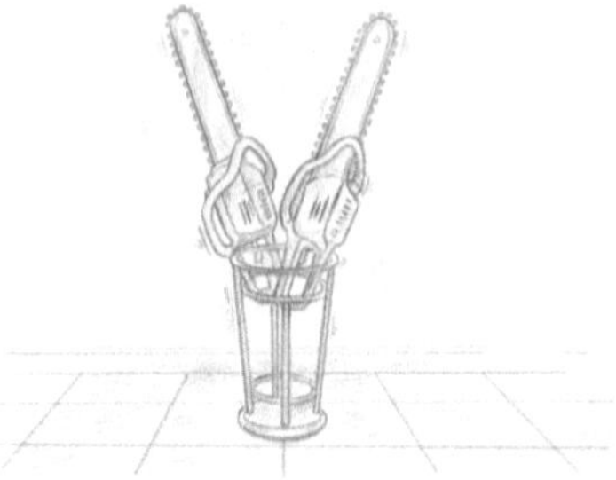

Kash has a rather brilliant—in my view—idea for how we can check the ten houses without looking like we're scoping them out for a later burglary or something. Since St. Mary's is a Catholic school, all of us kids need to sell boxes of candy to help raise money. So far, I haven't sold any and Barn ate several of his boxes, so his parents "bought" those by default. Kash, being on top of every assignment, has already sold all of hers. Since my mom is YouTubing at home and Barn's parents are at work, we ride to his house and pick up all his remaining candy.

"Can't I keep a few?"

Barn looks so morose that I agree to give him the ones my mom is planning to buy. That makes him happy.

Kash stuffs the boxes into her backpack and we set off. All the customers for those "ortho kicks" are elderly people—duh!

—and all of them are home at the first five houses we hit. Sadly, however, only one agrees to buy any candy and none of them look at all sketchy, at least to my well-trained "detective" eye.

Then we head to a house way up West 24th Street. It's a warm spring day here in Southern California, making the uphill bike ride all the more torturous, but I fare better than poor Barn. He's sweating like a sheepdog in the desert by the time we join Kash on the sidewalk in front of the house. She's barely winded.

"That was a fun ride," she announces smugly while Barn and me huff and puff our way to her side and dismount on shaky legs. At least mine are shaky. I can't tell about Barn because he's so doubled over trying to breathe that he doesn't do anything but suck in deep breaths like he's impersonating a heart-lung machine.

I toss Kash a major scowl, but my sweaty hair is covering half my face and she doesn't catch it. After several minutes of wheezing, I turn away from Kash's self-satisfied expression to study the house. It's one story, painted light blue with a small front yard surrounded by a low brick wall. There's no car in the driveway, and the separate garage in back—which I can see over the low gate—is closed.

Barn has finally stopped gasping and I eye him. "You good, Barn?"

He nods, even though I can tell he's not. Neither of us

wants to look even weaker than we already do in front of Kash.

There's a path to the front door from the driveway, so I wheel my bike forward and kick out the stand, leaving the bike beside a low hedge. Kash follows and Barn brings up the rear. With the bikes parked, Kash leads the way up to the door, box of candy in hand. I follow her, scanning the area for anything suspicious.

The front door has a square of glass at the height of a regular person (as opposed to hobbits like me), but fortunately Kash and Barn are tall enough to look inside. Kash depresses the doorbell button and an obnoxious sing-song version of *I've Been Workin' On the Railroad* wafts out of the house.

Barn and I exchange looks of dismay, while Kash just shrugs. The song ends and we wait. Nothing happens.

"Can you see anything inside?" I ask Kash, embarrassed again that I can't look for myself. I'll end up being the only detective in the world to need elevator shoes!

Kash leans closer and peers through the glass. She turns her head, apparently studying the interior. Then she gasps.

"What?"

I stand on tiptoes, but only the top of my head reaches the small window.

Kash steps back and ushers Barn forward. He presses his face against the glass so hard there's a print of his nose left behind when he pulls away.

Least it wasn't mine this time.

"I don't see anything," Barn says, looking at Kash in that clueless way he's mastered.

She sighs, as though the weight of the world is on her shoulders. "You didn't see the umbrella stand?"

"What about the umbrella stand?"

That's me, but Kash still stares at Barn, as though praying he'll figure it out, whatever "it" is.

"Yeah," Barn answers with a shrug. "What about it?"

"Did you see what was in it?"

I wanna scream at them to tell me what's up.

Barn shrugs again. "Two chainsaws, why?"

I gag and Kash rolls her eyes so hard I'm sure they'll never come back around.

Then she says to me, "There are chainsaws in the umbrella stand."

My heart pounds with excitement. "This is the place!"

Barn looks at me. "What makes you think so?"

I open my mouth to say something super snarky, but quickly shut it. Ari's lessons on self-control are working.

"Never mind. Let's just sneak around to the backyard and see if we can find anything."

"We're gonna go in their yard?" Barn's eyes are the size of ping pong balls.

"How else will we find any clues?" Kash says, taking the words right out of my mouth.

"We'll just look for anything sketch," I add.

"We could call Ari," Barn suggests.

I pause—the way Ari has taught me since I was seven—and consider that idea. It's the smart thing to do, for sure. And it's safer. But then my brain slips into Sherlock Holmes mode and I think, *there's nobody home, so how can it hurt to snoop around a bit?*

"I'll call him in a few," I say, scanning the street and the other houses to make sure we're not being watched. "After we check the backyard."

"But—"

"If we're gonna sneak around back, let's do it now before the whole neighborhood sees us," Kash snaps, her voice low and filled with irritation.

Barn backs down, like he always does with Kash.

I lead the way off the porch. Turning right, I slink along the side of the house toward the back gate. Needless to say, I'm too short to reach up and over for the latch and sheepishly step aside for Kash. She has the gate open in seconds and we duck through, closing and latching it so we're out of sight of the street.

The backyard is off to the right past the garage door. It's pretty ordinary. I scan it quickly, knowing I can "review the tape" later for more specific details. There's a ratty lawn that looks like it's tended by goats and some weed-infested flower beds, but no furniture and nothing that looks suspicious. Since we're short on time, I make for the back door. I grip the knob and twist. It turns and the door pops open. I glance back at the other two.

Barn shrugs, but Kash looks worried.

"Why would the door be unlocked if no one's home?" Her voice is barely a whisper.

I brush hair away from my eyes to study her face. "Maybe they forgot because this is a safe neighborhood," I suggest, knowing it's weak, but I really want to snoop around before calling Ari.

Kash gives me that look, the one that says, 'You're way too smart to believe that', which I normally like because it makes me feel less dorky, but now I ignore it because, well, I want to.

"Let's poke around a little," I whisper back. "At least snap some pics of those chainsaws for Ari."

She doesn't look happy but doesn't argue.

I ease the door open because, well, there might be a frothing pit bull waiting to attack. The hallway inside turns out to be empty. Okay, but the pit bull scenario *was* possible.

I creep forward onto a dingy tile floor. Barn trails me and Kash brings up the rear. We pass a door on the left that opens onto a kitchen. I glance in, but there's just the usual appliances and a small square table surrounded by four wooden chairs. I move further into the house toward a closed door on my right. I already know Kash thinks this is a bad idea, but I press my ear to the door and listen. There's nothing, so I turn the knob and pull it open. Stairs descend downward alongside walls made of brick. There's a light switch to my left and I flip it. Lights go on at the bottom of the stairs, but whatever is in this basement is hidden by the walls. We'll have to descend to the bottom to see what's there.

I pause and consider. Yes, we want photos of the chainsaws by the front door, but if I were doing something criminal, like I think these people are, I'd hide the evidence in the basement. But then, I'd also lock the door so no one—like three snooping middle school kids—could just walk down and find it. Even with all these very reasonable and logical doubts, my twelve-year-old brain just *has* to know what's down there. So, I descend the stairs.

Kash expels a major sigh of annoyance, but footsteps trail behind me on the creaky wood of the steps, so I know she's following.

As I reach the concrete floor at the bottom and step around the wall, I almost gag with shock. This isn't a basement with garden tools and other "normal" stuff. This is a dungeon! I mean, no joke, a real honest-to-goodness dungeon with shackles attached to the brick walls and one of those rack tables I've seen in movies that're used to stretch people until they cough up important information.

"Whoa," says Barn as he steps to my side.

"What *is* this place?" Kash stares at the shackles in disbelief.

My gaze sweeps the room, allowing my brain time to "film" everything, and then I spot a table on the other side of the rack. There's chemistry equipment, like beakers and test tubes, and beside those are bottles of colored liquid. And scattered on the table are broken pieces of... hearing aids! I lurch forward and give the rack a wide berth as I make a beeline for the hearing aids.

There's a hammer and chisel beside them and I can tell each pair of aids has been broken apart with care. Kash and Barn join me.

"Somebody had a temper tantrum," Barn jokes and I almost toss back a snarky response but bite my tongue.

Instead, I glance at Kash. "Whadda ya think, Kash?"

Without touching anything, she studies the broken pieces. "Looks like they're searching for something hidden in a hearing aid."

"I agree," I say, feeling good about this discovery. "Question is, did they find it?"

I pull out my phone and snap some pictures of the table and the broken hearing aids.

"Well, well, what have we here?"

It's a voice that *doesn't* belong to us.

Chapter 5

Barn, They're Gonna Kill Us

I spin around. Barn and Kash do the same. A white-haired old man stands beside the torture rack holding up a chainsaw. He's short and shaped kind of like a turnip, but he's gripping the heavy-looking chainsaw in one wrinkled hand like it weighs nothing.

Kash raises her fists into a fighting stance, while Barn lets his mouth drop into an "O" of surprise. I'm so startled for a moment that I don't answer.

"Billy, you down there? There's bikes in the driveway."

It's a woman's voice, old and scratchy, by the sound of it, calling from the top of the stairs.

The old man glances back. "Down here, Polly. We got us some uninvited guests."

I note that Kash is ready to spring into action, but she looks understandably concerned at the prospect of taking on a chainsaw. Still, I'm thinking, the guy is super old, so Kash should be faster, right?

Tromping steps descend the stairs, fast and strong, not slow and lumbering like I expected from hearing the voice. An old lady appears from around the wall at the foot of the stairs and hurries forward. No joke. She practically runs. I glance down at her shoes—they're the same orthopedic ones I traced to Mr. Loafer's place!

The lady is skinny, like she might break in two at the slightest push, and her white hair is tucked up under a hair-net. But her eyes are fiercely alert and her movements agile, like she's a young person pretending to be old. What's going on?

The old man fills her in on how he found us down here, while my mind races with ideas on how we can escape.

The woman smirks, but her wrinkles make it look like she's choking on a prune. "I guess we have to kill 'em, Billy."

"You sure?"

"We can't leave 'em here. Dr. Drug wants us on the island ASAP."

The old guy frowns. "What about the hearing aids?"

"He said forget 'em for now. The rocket is almost ready."

I can't let all this go unchallenged. "Wait. You work for a guy named Dr. Drug? What kind of lame name is that?"

The old man chuckles. "That's what I told him."

The woman "shushes" him and studies me. "It's a fake

name. Even we don't know his true identity, but he's one of the most powerful men on the planet."

"Maybe, but not very imaginative," I snort, hoping my false bravado will lower their guard.

The old lady grins. Her teeth look yellowed and crooked. "Maybe not, but we are. Most people would just shoot you, but we're going to carve you up with this chainsaw."

I gulp and glance at Kash, since she's the only one who knows how to fight. But I see right away her martial arts classes never dealt with a close-quarters chainsaw attack.

The woman glances at the man. "Billy, start the chainsaw."

The man grins and reaches with his free hand for a pull cord on the side of the saw. He yanks it hard—harder than I'd think possible with such frail-looking arms. The saw roars to deafening life and the chain begins spinning.

"I have a proposal," I blurt out as the old man takes an ominous step forward.

The woman raises what used to be eyebrows, but now there are just a few wisps of white hair straddling the ridges above her eyes. "Billy, stop the chainsaw."

Billy releases his finger from the "trigger" and the saw slows to an idle.

"What is your proposal, boy?" The old lady folds her arms across her chest in an 'I'm waiting to be amused' gesture.

"You don't really wanna kill cute, innocent kids, do you?"

I flash what I hope is a good version of my "cute" Muppit Boy look.

The man grimaces and the woman grunts.

"Cute? With that nose?" She shakes her head in amazement. "Billy, start the chainsaw."

The man hits the trigger and the saw thunders back to life.

I know I'm beet red, despite my shaking knees, but I swallow my pride. "Wait. I have another idea."

The old lady sighs heavily. It sounds like a dying air conditioner. "Billy, stop the chainsaw."

He returns the saw to idle mode.

"Well?" The lady studies my face more intently. That can't be good.

"How about you let us go and we won't turn you over to the police?"

Okay, fear kind of has my brain wrapped in cellophane.

She shakes her head again, clearly disgusted with my stupidity. But then her eyes bug out of her head. Seriously. They practically hit me in the face.

"You're Muppit Boy! I knew I recognized you!" She grabs the man's arm. "It's him, Billy!"

Oh, no...

The man squints in the dim lighting. "Move the hair aside, sonny."

With a trembling hand, I slide the bangs off my face.

Now I see both people clearly, without a screen of black hair in front of my glasses.

The man looks unsure. "I don't think so, Polly. Look at that nose. It's even bigger than Muppit Boy's."

Kash expels an angry breath, while I want to disappear into the floor.

"You old fool," the woman says, punching him on the arm. "Muppit Boy hasn't been on that show for two years. Kids grow and so do their noses."

My ears are burning, not just with embarrassment, but with rage.

The woman steps closer and studies my face some more. "You *are* Muppit Boy, aren't you?"

That's it. I'm done being the town joke!

"Billy," I snarl, "start the chainsaw."

The man's bushy gray eyebrows shoot up in surprise and then he laughs. It sounds like smoke belching from a car's exhaust pipe. "You're Muppit Boy, all right. I recognize that snarky sense of humor." I wasn't joking about the chainsaw, but I don't get a chance to say so because the old man continues. "I swear, my favorite episode was when you was maybe six years old. You was standing at the open refrigerator staring at some cake and the door closed right on your nose. My dentures near fell out, I laughed so hard."

Humiliation has completely taken over and I almost hope they *do* kill me!

The old lady moves closer and Kash darts out with one

fist. The lady jumps back like a gazelle and my embarrassment is momentarily forgotten.

How did she do that?

"Don't try any Bruce Lee stuff on me, little lady," the woman rasps, once again beside the old man. "I'm stronger than I look."

I'm beginning to realize there's a lot about these two that doesn't add up.

"Can we have an autograph, Muppit Boy?" The old lady's tone sounds like she happened to meet me at the mall instead of planning to murder me.

I rear back. "Of course not!"

Barn gives me a 'look.' "Come on, Mo, don't be selfish. They're *fans*."

I've known Barn since preschool and he's not as dumb as people think. He's clearly stalling for time, which is pretty smart, so I play along.

"Barn, they're gonna kill us."

He shrugs. "So? That'll just make your autograph worth more on eBay."

"Barney!" Kash raises a fist. She doesn't know Barn the way I do, so she thinks he's serious.

Barn leans away quickly. "Just trying to help. Maybe they'll let us go."

"Fat chance, sonny," snaps the old lady.

Barn glances at me. "Come on, Mo. You can use that new pen Kash gave you."

I want to grin so broadly my nose might even look smaller as a result. But I keep my cool and turn to the old couple. "Okay. You have a printer upstairs?"

"Course we do," the man snaps indignantly. "You think we're old or something?"

I bite my tongue on that one. "Uh, anyway, if you wanna take my picture and print it out, I'll sign it."

The old lady claps with glee. "This is so exciting! You're the biggest celebrity we've ever met."

"You don't get out much, do you?" I can't help it. The sarcasm drips from every word.

She laughs. "You're too modest, Muppit Boy. Dr. Drug is a huge fan. He'll be jealous that we got to meet you and he didn't."

I'm sure Mom will be thrilled to know she has a super villain fanboy. Sensing that this Dr. Drug is the main dude behind everything, I try another stalling tactic. "I don't mind meeting him."

"That would be a nice surprise for the boss," she says, her face falling slightly, "but we need to dispose of you here. He doesn't like dead bodies in his lab."

She reaches into her billowy grandma dress, where she must have pockets, and pulls out a smartphone. She points to Barn. "You, fat boy, over there." She indicates an area near the brick wall.

Barn looks offended, but shuffles to the indicated spot.

Then the woman wiggles her finger at Kash. "You, girly, will take the photo. No funny business."

The man holds up the chainsaw, one hand on the trigger.

"Turn that off first," I insist.

The old man glances at the lady and she nods. He flicks the switch to off and the idling drone turns to silence.

The old woman extends her phone toward Kash. Kash glances at me and I shrug. She steps up, snatches the phone from the woman, and steps back.

The woman waves me forward.

Trying to act casual so they won't get suspicious, I approach with feigned confidence. "Where do you want me?"

"Right in the middle," the woman says, indicating a space between her and the man. "Oh, and drop the messenger bag to the floor."

I tilt my head quizzically. "I don't have any weapons in it, if that's what you think."

"If I carry a chainsaw in my purse, who knows what a kid like you might have. Drop it."

I slip off my bag and toss it to the floor.

"Now, in the middle." She grins like this is the best day of her life.

It's *definitely* not mine.

Eyeing the chainsaw blade, I take the last few steps so my trembling body is between two people who plan to kill me. I'm not sure I can describe that feeling but scared out of my freaking mind kind of comes close.

The woman puts her arm around my shoulders like we're best friends. "C'mon, Billy, lean in."

The man presses close to me, his left arm around my shoulders.

"Put the saw right up to his throat, Billy, like we mean business."

I flinch as the blade of a very deadly garden tool that could lop off my head rests against the tender flesh of my throat. I'm afraid to swallow.

Kash holds up the phone.

"Now smile!" the lady admonishes.

I dare not even glance in either direction, so my smile probably looks like I'm gritting my teeth. I feel wrinkly fingers brushing against my forehead and pushing my hair aside.

"That's better," the woman says smugly. "We want to see the nose."

I want to scream but dare not budge. Kash snaps off a few photos and then the chainsaw blade eases away from my throat. I'm weak in the knees as I lurch back to Kash's side. Seriously, my legs feel like rubber and I'm quivering all over.

The woman reaches for the phone and examines the photos. "*Ooooh,* they're perfect. I'll run up and print one. Billy, run the chainsaw while I'm gone. Don't want them trying anything."

She sprints across the basement to the stairs. That's the truth. She *sprints* and then takes the stairs two at a time.

My terror at nearly being sliced and diced like a tree

stump is gone in an instant and my Sherlock curiosity kicks into high gear. Even the chainsaw roaring to life doesn't faze me. I glance at Kash and see that she's as mystified as I am. Even Barn looks confused.

The noisy saw somewhat disrupts my thoughts because I picture it slicing through my neck, but I try to wrap my brain around how these old people—who are clearly old and not in some kind of stage make-up—can move around like people in their twenties. It makes no sense.

The old lady is back faster than I'd have imagined, holding out a glossy 8x10 photograph. "Kill the saw, Billy."

He does.

"I just spoke to the boss," she says to Billy, keeping her eye on me. "He couldn't believe it when I told him who broke into the house." She faces me straight on. "But he wasn't surprised. Said he expected no less from Muppit Boy."

I affect my most sarcastic expression. "Seriously? I'm being complimented by a guy who can't even think up a good villain name?"

She grins, spreading her wrinkles outward like cracks in window. "You can tell him that yourself. We're bringing you with us. Your friends, too."

"That doesn't sound good," Barn mutters.

"It probably won't be for you," she agrees. "But the boss has plans for Muppit Boy. I don't know what for sure, but I got me an idea."

The ominous tone in her voice makes me shiver, but I force myself to stay calm.

We need to escape.

Now.

"Um," I begin, pointing at the photo. "How'd it come out?"

With a grin, she steps closer and hands me the picture, warily keeping out of reach of Kash's clenched fists. "It's perfect."

I take the picture and almost gag. In the shot, I'm grimacing, but the two oldsters look giddy with joy. I wanna kick Kash for framing the angle so my nose looks almost 3D! Remembering that this is all a ploy to escape, I slip the trick pen from my pocket and eye the two adults.

"Uh, what do you want me to write?"

The woman rubs her hands together with excitement. "How about, 'To Polly and Billy, with love—"

"Wait a minute," says the man, stepping to her side. "Why does your name go first? I'm just as big a fan as you."

They are both huddled close to me and the photo, like they don't trust me to write what they say. But it's all good. I need them close for the pen to work. Kash didn't tell me its range.

"Because it was my idea to get his autograph!" snaps the woman. "Now shut up and let me think." Her face lights up. "I've got it."

I poise the pen over the photo and wait.

"To Polly and Billy, with love. Then sign it 'Nosily yours, Muppit Boy'."

I rear back in horror. "Nosily yours?"

The woman smiles broadly. "It's perfect, isn't it?"

A kid can only take so much. "No way."

The woman indicates the chainsaw.

I shake my head, my bangs swishing back and forth like a mop. "I won't write that. It's too cruel."

Kash nudges me and I look over.

"Just write it, Mo."

Her gaze flicks to the pen clutched tightly between my thumb and forefinger, and my body relaxes slightly, my anger subsiding.

Control, my brain tells me, like Ari says.

I take a deep breath and let it out. I aim the pen at the photo, pausing for dramatic effect. It works. The old people lean in even closer. I pretend to click the pen, acting like it doesn't work.

"Good one, Kash," I say, snark in full force. "You gave me a pen that doesn't work."

She pretends to be offended. "It worked for me. Give it a shake."

That's my cue. I turn the pen over and shake it. At the same time, I depress the clicker. Black ink streams from the end of the pen – right into the faces of our captors. They cry out in surprise and the man drops the chainsaw. I leap back and it bounces inches from where my foot had been. The old folks claw at their eyes, temporarily blinded.

"Now!" I dart around the moaning adults and run for the stairs.

Barn and Kash are right behind me.

"Come back here, you little creep!"

That's the old lady's voice, but I don't wait to see what they're doing. I'm up the stairs and into the hall within seconds.

Kash practically shoves Barn after me and then she slams the door.

I look, but there's no lock. "C'mon!"

I sprint down the hall toward the front door. The deadbolt is locked, but I twist it to the right and pull open the door. I hear from behind us, "They're getting away!" and then footsteps pounding up the dungeon stairs.

I'm through the door in a flash, the others behind me. For a big kid, Barn can sure move when he's scared. We're into the driveway and onto our bikes before I realize I still have the photo in my hands. Realizing that it's evidence and I no longer have my messenger bag, I shove it into the front of my pants, up and under my shirt.

I barely notice that there're two motorcycles parked in the driveway as I kick off and start down the street, my legs pumping faster than ever in my life. Barn rolls along on my right and Kash on my left. We're pretty high up in San Pedro and 24th Street slopes downward at a steep angle, so we quickly pick up speed and leave the house behind.

Chapter 6

You Could Get Killed!

"What now?" That's Kash, as we pedal furiously down the steeply inclined street.

"I'm calling Ari!"

I release one hand from the handlebars and slip out my phone, sticking it onto its holder. "Call Ari on cell!"

"Calling Ari on cell," wafts out of my phone in that melodious computerized voice.

As the call connects, I have to keep whipping my head back to keep the hair away from my glasses.

Ari's smiling face appears on my screen. "Hey, Mo, what's up?"

"Ari, I'm in trouble!"

I'm about to say more when from behind me, in the distance, an engine guns. Glancing back, I can still see the blue house way up the hill. A motorcycle zooms out of the driveway. The rider wears a helmet, but I recognize the dress – it's the old lady! The cycle roars after us and I whip my head back around.

"Mo, what's going on?" Ari sounds worried.

"No time to explain. The chainsaw clown and her partner are chasing us."

"What?"

"We're on our bikes, but they have motorcycles. We'll never outrun 'em!"

"Okay, Mo, stay calm, like I taught you." I know he's afraid for me, but his voice sounds rock solid, just what I need right now. "Where are you?"

I glance around at the street signs whizzing past. "We're headed down West Twenty-Fourth Street, just passing Walker." I glance back. Our pursuers are gaining. "They're getting closer, Ari!"

"I'm on it. Keep this line open so I can hear what's happening."

"You got it." I look over at Kash. She's staring at me. "Did you hear?"

"Yeah," she calls back against the wind. "But we can't outride motorcycles, Mo!"

"Mo, they're coming!"

I glance over at Barn, and he looks panic-stricken. His hands grip his handlebars with knuckle-whitening intensity as his thick legs pump and pedal for all they're worth.

"Ari's on it!" I call back.

But Ari isn't here and we are, so the immediate solution has to come from us. I look over at Kash. When it comes to self-defense and martial arts, she's fearless. But her face is twisted with terror. She's not even trying to hide it. Looks like the solution has to come from me.

My legs are already burning from the exertion of pedaling so hard. I look ahead and see Leland Street fast approaching. I know there's an alley behind some houses half a block down Leland. If our pursuers don't see us swing into a turn, we might be able to hide in that alley.

"Hug the sidewalk!" I shout at the others. "Sharp right on Leland, then left down the alley! We gotta be fast or they'll see us!"

I look back over my shoulder. A moving van is turning onto 24th from Walker Street. It will block the oldsters for a few seconds while they veer around it. I turn back. Leland looms twenty feet ahead. My bike wheels hug the curb, the others in line behind me. Then the corner's there and I swerve sharply to the right. Not being an X Games wanna-be, I almost fly right off the bike as it skids on the asphalt, and I fight to keep it upright. The alley approaches on my left. With no time to look back, I swing a wide turn to the left and sail down the empty alley that flanks the back fences of private homes.

I hear Barn cry out in fear, but there's no crash so I figure he made the turn without running into anything. Kash is more coordinated than both of us, so I know she's okay.

"Mo, where are you now?"

Ari's voice startles me. He's issuing orders in the background, and I think I hear a car start, but fleeing for my life kind of holds my attention.

"Alley between... Twenty-Fourth... and Twenty-Fifth," I call out breathlessly, glancing back to see if the motorcyclists caught what we did.

The alley is empty.

"I think we... lost 'em for right now."

"We're setting up a roadblock at Twenty-Fourth and Gaffey and black and whites are on the move in your direction. Any description of the perps or their bikes?"

I'm still cruising at a pretty fast speed but take a moment and rewind my brain to when I first spotted the motorcycles.

"One's on a red bike and the other on blue. The lady's wearing a billowy dress and a helmet with lightning bolts."

"That's my boy!"

Ari's voice is so filled with pride that I momentarily forget how it's my stupidity that might get us killed.

Since Ari's going to be at 24th and Gaffey, I decide to head that way, too. We're coming up to a T where this alley is cut through by another one, so we'll have to turn right or left.

Despite my burning lungs, I call out, "We're going left, to Twenty-Fourth and Gaffey!"

"You sure?" Kash's fishtail braid flops around behind her like a real fish out of water.

"Ari's there!"

She nods.

I glance at Barn. "You okay, Barn?"

"Do I look okay?" His face is twisted with fear, even more than the time I convinced him to climb a telephone pole when we were six and he got stuck up there.

"Ari will save us," I call back, but Barn doesn't look a smidgen less afraid. I don't blame him. We need to *get* to Ari first.

Approaching police sirens rip through the quiet afternoon. I swing left at the end of the alley and then ease up on my pedaling as I approach 24th Street because there's a long line of cars moving sluggishly in the direction of Gaffey. They all have their headlights on. I slow to a stop and the others stop on either side of me.

"What's...going on?" I struggle to regain my breath.

Kash looks over at me, not even winded. "Looks like a funeral procession."

"That could be good for us," I gasp, eyeing the steady stream of cars. They can't be going more than ten miles per hour. "They can give us cover."

"What if they run us down?"

I turn to Barn with my mouth open. "Barn, even *I* can out-pedal them."

He looks dubious but doesn't argue. I wave them forward and then follow, watching as Kash and Barn pass between two of the vehicles and move out of sight onto 24th Street. I pause. Having seen no sign of the motorcycle pursuit for a few minutes, I ease forward, preparing to dart between two cars. Just as I'm turning the corner, a roar fills my ears and I whip my head around in shock.

The old man bears down on me, waving the roaring chainsaw like it's a toy. I press hard with my right foot onto the bike pedal, but of course it slips off and the bike starts to tip. I push against the asphalt, slam my foot back onto the pedal and pump with every ounce of energy I have as the deafening rumble closes in from behind. I'm just about to swing a hard-right turn onto 24th alongside a black SUV when I feel a jolt at my rear tire and the bike veers sharply, slamming against the SUV and causing the woman in the passenger seat to scream in surprised shock. I turn my head to see my rear tire exposed and the wheel cover spinning backwards along the street. And the motorcyclist is right behind me, chainsaw roaring!

Kash and Barn are on the other side of the cars. I scream at them to pedal faster as I pump myself away from the SUV, cut in front of the car that precedes it, and sail out into the oncoming traffic lane.

The SUV driver calls out, "Hey, kid, get back here!"

But I don't even turn. The motorcycle is still in pursuit, copying my movements and eliciting another shout from the same driver. The police sirens increase in volume, but no cruisers are in sight as I zoom past Alma Street to join Kash and Barn. They have their heads down against the wind and focus on pedaling. I risk a glance back.

The red motorcycle with the woman on it swings onto 24th from the opposite side of Alma and joins her partner. We're in trouble. Gaffey is blocks away and the cops aren't here yet!

"Split up!" I scream at the others.

Kash glances over and I know she's going to argue, so I call out, "Kash, you go right on the next street." I turn to Barn. "Barn, go left. They can't catch all of us!"

"I'm not gonna leave you," Kash yells against the wind.

"It's the only way!"

Even at the speed we're moving, I can see she doesn't want to leave me. Barn is so scared he'll do whatever I say, but Kash is a fighter through and through.

I look ahead as Meyler Street rapidly approaches. "Now!"

I fly through that intersection and note in my peripheral vision that my friends veer off in their assigned directions. As I approach the hearse at the head of the procession, I glance back over my shoulder. Both cyclists are chasing *me*!

I face forward and note the hearse looming on my right. I get an idea and hope I'm coordinated enough to pull it off. The old man with the chainsaw is closing fast, barely fifteen feet back. I veer sharply to the right to zip between the back of the hearse and the car following. As I do, I fling out my left arm and scrabble for the rear door latch on the hearse. With only seconds to grab it, I feel my fingers slip around the silver handle. I yank it down and pull.

The long rear door swings outward and I nearly lose my balance as I let go and slap my hand back onto my handlebars. I swerve and bounce up onto the sidewalk and fight to keep upright. From behind, I hear a loud thud mixed with the roaring of the saw. I glance back in time to see the cycle slamming into the open hearse door and tearing it from its moorings. The chainsaw goes flying and the old man, whose face is obscured by the helmet, cries out in fury as he tumbles off the bike. He lands hard onto his back while the speeding bike pushes the hearse door before it, slams through a wooden fence and vanishes into someone's front yard.

I pedal into the street ahead of the hearse and take another look back. The old lady slows her motorcycle near the old man on the ground and I think I'm home free when I'm stunned to see the man getting nimbly to his feet, apparently not hurt in the least!

What's going on here?

That raspy voice, muffled beneath the helmet, snaps, "I'm fine. Get Muppit Boy!"

The woman revs her motorcycle engine in pursuit.

Now I'm really scared. Are these people indestructible or something? I pedal with frantic desperation. My long bangs are damp with sweat that drips into my eyes. The roar of the cycle grows louder. But so do the police sirens. I'm nearing

Cabrillo Street when two black and whites round the corners from both directions and speed up 24th right at me!

I squeeze my brakes. Nothing happens. I pump the brake handles rapidly. Nothing. The steep hill is increasing my speed and the cop cars are bearing down. I glance at my back wheel and groan. The brakes are gone! They must've been sheared off in the chainsaw attack. I look back up the street. It's clear the old lady has seen the police because she's stopped her motorcycle like she's debating her chances.

I can't worry about her. I turn around. The cop cars are almost on me. I veer to the right and into the other lane. I suddenly remember my phone and hope the call is still connected.

"Ari, my brakes are out!"

There's crackling from my phone speaker, then, "What did you say, Mo? I can see you now."

I look ahead. Several blocks further down the hill is a line of police cars, lights flashing, blocking Gaffey Street. If I keep going, I'll slam right into them.

"Ari, my brakes are out. I can't stop!"

"What!"

"The old guy cut off my brakes with the chainsaw!"

I know I sound frantic because, well, I *am*!

I hear an unfamiliar voice over the hissing wind on the phone, "Did he say a chainsaw?"

"Do we have a net, anything to stop a bike with no brakes?" Ari sounds frantic, too.

I'm too far away to see his face, but he's pacing back and forth in front of the cars. Men in uniform run and pop the trunks of police cruisers while Ari stops and stares up at me. My heart is in my throat as the speed of my bike increases, and I'm not even pedaling!

"Hang on, Mo!" comes through the phone.

If I weren't about to have a heart attack, I'd shout back that I can't do anything *but* hang on.

Then another voice says, "We don't have anything that will stop a bike, Detective."

"That's my boy out there!"

I might be about to die, but my heart swells momentarily. Then my blood freezes when Ari starts walking up 24th in my direction.

"Mo, steer your bike right at me. I'm going to snatch you off as it passes."

"No!" I can't help but shout. "You could get killed!"

Ari stands in the middle of the street. I glance back and see that the woman and her motorcycle are gone. So are the cop cars. The people from the funeral procession are all out of their vehicles, frozen like an exhibit at the Natural History Museum. Some have their phones out, while others hold a hand to their mouths in horror.

I turn back to Ari. He's right in my path, no more than a hundred feet away. I'm barreling down the hill now, faster than I've ever gone on my bike. If Ari grabs for me, he'll be killed for sure. Tears spill from my eyes against my will and are flung back along my face by the wind.

"Ari, I'm scared."

"I know you are, Mo," Ari says in that calm, strong voice that's comforted me since I was seven. "But I can do this."

"Please, Ari...." I'm crying now, solidifying my dweeb reputation for all to see. But I can't help it. "I don't want you getting hurt!"

"I don't care about me. I'm going to save you. Now keep coming. I'm putting the phone in my pocket now."

Before I can respond, he slips the phone into his pants pocket and spreads his arms wide. He crouches, like he used to do when we wrestled on my back lawn and he taught me a few moves from his high school days.

I'm seventy-five feet back, now sixty, now fifty... I can't stop crying because I know I'm going to hurt the person I love most in this world, and I've never even told him how much he means to me.

I note his determined face, his taut body, crouched like a wild animal preparing to spring at its dinner, arms reaching for me.

I want to close my eyes, but I can't. My brain registers the other cops standing by their cars gazing up at the scene in silence. There're no traffic sounds because they have Gaffey blocked. There's only wind whipping past my face and my Big Brother reaching out to save me because I can't save myself.

I'm twenty feet away when I'm hit with a sudden gust of wind from above and I hear a powerful flapping sound, like the world's largest sheet being whipped around in a gale.

I start to look up when something thick and sharp grabs me around my upper arms, right near the shoulders, and then I'm not on the bike anymore! I'm rising into the air with alarming speed!

Chapter 7

You're My Boy

Ari looks up, his face twisted with fear. "Mo!"

Then he leaps to one side as my bicycle rips past him and slams into one of the cop cars so hard the front wheel bends at a forty-five-degree angle and the bike flips up and over the car. Cops leap aside and I watch my trusty old bike land in a battered heap in the middle of Gaffey Street.

"Mo!"

Ari has both hands cupped around his mouth as he calls out, but I'm at least thirty feet in the air and dangling helplessly from...what? I was so scared for Ari I forgot to even look up. I tilt my head back, forcing my glasses to retreat back up my nose where they belong, and my breathing almost stops as I behold the biggest freaking bird I've ever seen! I'm not kidding. The wingspan has to be ten feet! The curved beak is gigantic, and its body must be five feet long! I can't really get a good look at the claws that grip me, but based on the beak, I don't think I want to. The bird just glides through the air like it doesn't have a care in the world, except it's carrying me to who knows where and I'm panicking like crazy!

I look down and spot Ari sprinting to an unmarked car mixed in among the black and whites, and the other cops are jumping into their cars, too. It's obvious they're going to pursue me, but to where? I even see Barn and Kash pedaling down 24th, following me. I've passed over Gaffey by now and the bird continues flapping lazily out toward the ocean. I experience another stab of panic to the heart – what if it drops me somewhere? The ocean would be okay, if, you know, I don't fall too far. High diving was never my thing. But if it lets me go over land, I'll be flatter than one of my mother's pancakes.

As terrified as I am, it's also a crazy, wild feeling to dangle in mid-air, soaring above the roofs of houses like a superhero. My lifelong obsession with flying has finally come true and the reality is exhilarating! For a shrimpy kid like me, who's always had to look up at just about everything, it's both scary and exciting. And the world doesn't seem so frightening from up here. It's actually very pretty; even the different colored rooftops are attractive. And I never much noticed trees before. But from up here, seeing those green-leaved branches reaching for me like grasping hands sends my ADHD into overdrive. I have a weird feeling that if I don't die, this experience will be the most incredible of my life.

I glance back as best I can. In the distance, I spot Ari's car and the black and whites leaving Kash and Barn in the dust and roaring down 24th in pursuit. But the bird banks left and soars above another street, still in the direction of the ocean.

I know it's stupid, but I'm a middle schooler so I look upward and shout, "Hey, bird, where're you taking me?"

The bird cocks its massive head and one of those swirling black eyes seems to fix on me. As though it understood my question, it screeches like a chicken on steroids and then looks straight ahead again, like it wants to show me something. Ahead, near the beach—I can't estimate how far because everything looks different up here—is Fort MacArthur, an old army base now used by the Air Force. It's a series of large buildings with nice-looking red rooftops and huge expanses of green grass. I went there once on a school field trip and it's a really cool place that goes all the way back to 1914, if my video recorder brain is working at the moment.

I don't see anyone walking around as the gigantic bird banks right and soars over a wall into the complex. I'm still twenty feet above the roofs, but my stomach suddenly flies into my throat as the bird begins dropping. A large expanse of grass looms ever closer and the bird still doesn't slow. I hold my breath and snap my eyes shut. I just know we're going to crash! Wind whips my hair as the wings beat wildly with that sheet-flapping sound and then...my feet gently touch the ground and my knees buckle. The bird holds me securely until I'm down in a shaking heap on the grass, and then the claws unclasp.

I'm free.

I roll onto my back to catch my breath and find myself inches from an extra-long snout and thick neck. The beak is sharply curved downward like gardening shears, and I know this bird could snap my boney wrist with one bite. The wings are pulled in now and I vaguely notice that the feathers are multi-colored and don't all look like they belong on the same bird. But they're beautiful. The bird, however, is pretty ugly. Reminds me of a vulture I saw on TV.

I sit up because the bird isn't doing anything sketchy. It just stands on those massive, clawed feet and gazes at me, like it knows who I am.

"Uh, thanks," I say because I want to hear something.

I guess there's not much going on today at Fort MacArthur because no one has come out to see why an enormous bird just dropped a kid onto their front lawn.

The bird *squawks* again and leans in close to my face. It smells like it's got super bad breath and I want to flinch away, but it just saved my life and I don't want to be rude, so I sit with my hands behind me on the grass and don't move. It moves its head closer. I hold my breath. That beak could rip my face off. But it doesn't. It touches my nose so gently my eyes burn with tears. The beak grazes my nose softly, back and forth, and I understand that this is the bird's way of expressing friendship.

The nose rubbing continues for a few seconds and the bird makes a light gurgling sound from deep inside before pulling its head back to study me. There's a long moment where we just gaze at one another, and I experience an odd sense of camaraderie, a genuine connection I don't even have with my friends. Then, with a swoop of its massive wings, the bird lifts off, blasting wind into my face and drying the tears glistening in my eyes. I watch my savior soar off in the direction of the harbor.

I can't really describe my feelings because I'm so confused by everything that's happened.

Police sirens rip through the air, moving rapidly in my direction. Moments later, Ari's black sedan roars up the street, followed by several cop cars. Ari's out of the car almost before it rolls to a stop and pelts across the expanse of grass toward me.

My legs still tremble, and I search the sky for the bird that saved me, but it's gone. Then I'm engulfed in Ari's long, strong arms. He's on his knees practically crushing me with his hug, his beard rubbing my face in a way that's comforting. I wrap my arms around him, shivering with leftover remnants of fear.

"Are you all right, Mo?"

I nod into his shoulder as cops and random people run toward us. I hear a *whup whup whup* sound from above and glance up at a news helicopter aiming a camera down at us. How long has that been there?

Suddenly, I'm embarrassed by Ari hugging me in public, even though I know I shouldn't be. Ari taught me long ago that the "Boy Code" was written by idiots—you know that code, the one that says boys can't cry or show affection or hug each other? I know he's right, and normally I try not to care about it, but now with a crowd of people surrounding me and a news camera filming, I feel exposed and vulnerable.

"I'm okay, Ari," I assure him. "Thank you for trying to save me."

He releases the hug and pulls back so we can make eye contact. He looks scared and happy at the same time. "You're my boy."

Another Boy Code violation assails me and my eyes well again with tears as he helps me to my feet. I fight them back. "Are Barn and Kash okay?"

"Yes. The cyclists escaped, but we're combing the city for them."

I confess, I'm still a bit shaky, but everything that's happened in the past couple of hours starts replaying in my mind.

"They're really old, Ari, but strong, and can run fast and ride those bikes. They were gonna cut us up with chainsaws until this Dr. Drug guy said to kidnap us instead!"

Ari frowns, but Carter whistles in derision as he saunters up.

I turn to Ari's partner and glower. Remembering the photo, I smugly reach under my shirt. I can't find it and momentarily panic. Instinctively, I shove my hand down my pants, realizing way too late that people are filming me with their phones.

Carter's eyes shoot up in shocked amusement.

Ari clears his throat. "Uh, Mo...."

I know my face is beet red, but I don't care once my fingers feel the photo down in my underwear. I yank it out fast. It's bent, but I hand it to Ari in triumph, while casting Carter my best version of a smirk.

Ari almost gasps but keeps his composure. I know it's because of the chainsaw at my throat. He hands the picture off to Carter without turning away and then leans in to examine my neck. He touches a spot and I wince.

"There's a small cut."

I know he wants to say more, but won't embarrass me, especially when Carter grunts as he views the photo.

Ari stands and snatches back the photo. "You're braver than most adults, Mo, and very clear headed. Good call on saving this." He hands the photo to one of the uniformed officers. "Get this on the wire. APB for these two."

The officer takes the photo. "Yes, sir."

"And blot out Mo's face," Ari adds before the officer can turn away. "He's been through enough."

"Yes, sir," the officer repeats and then sprints back toward one of the black and whites.

Ari scans the crowd and notes the helicopter hovering overhead. The rotors are beginning to annoy me with their incessant noise. Ari wraps an arm around my shoulders.

"Let's go to the station to debrief. I'll have some men pick up Barn and Kash."

I nearly sag with relief. The weight of everyone staring pulls me down and I shake my head so that my bangs cover my face.

"Thanks, Ari." It still amazes me how he so often knows what I need before I do.

He leads me through the gathered crowd of people. Most are holding up phones. Where did so many people come from so quickly? Thankfully, I'm into Ari's front seat within minutes and then he's behind the wheel. He banks a U-Turn and heads downtown.

Chapter 8

I Am Not Muppit Boy!

Ari doesn't ask any questions on the ride to the station. He understands that I'm rewinding my brain through everything that happened this afternoon so I can give him a full report. Of course, Mom had left a dozen messages on his phone. Mine probably got trashed with my bike, but we don't head back there to check. Ari assures Mom that I'm fine and to meet us at the station. He hands me the phone and Mom's frantic voice pours forth, "Oh, Elmo, you're really all right?"

I can tell she's been crying and that makes me feel even worse about my "death of Muppit Boy" remark this morning.

"Yeah, Mom, I'm good. Really." I hear her choking back a sob and my stomach clenches. "Uh, how did you know something happened to me?"

"Mo, it's all over the news," she gasps back, regaining

control of her voice. "When I saw that bird grab you and fly away, I almost died from fright!"

I feel the color drain from my face. It's been on the news already? And there's video of me dangling like a frightened rag doll?

"I'm sorry, Mom." That's all I can think of to say, but then add, "I love you."

I hear that choking sound again. "I love you more. I'm on my way."

Her car engine revs, and the call clicks off. I hold onto the phone and resume my rewind.

The Harbor Community Police Station is a straight shot north on Pacific Avenue, right near the concrete monstrosity known as the 110 Freeway. It's a cool-looking, modern building with three floors, lots of windows, three tall flag poles, and the words "Los Angeles Police Department HARBOR DIVISION" above the front entrance.

I sit in my favorite revolving chair in Ari's third-floor office and detail everything that happened since he left my house this morning. He records it all on a tape recorder and takes notes, too. He never interrupts once because, now that I'm calm and rewound, I give very clear details about all that I saw and heard. It takes about twenty minutes.

Ari's whole body goes stiff when I tell him about the chainsaw stuff. I even tell him that, for a brief moment, I almost wanted that old man to slice me up. When I do, Ari gets that 'don't you even think of it' look I've seen a few times over the years, and a stab of remorse pierces my heart for causing him so much worry. I don't even mention the "nosily yours" part because that's just so beyond humiliating I can't even think about it without crying.

The door flies open and Mom rushes in, followed closely by Kash and Barn. Mom's hair looks disheveled, and her clothes are a hodgepodge, I guess because she left in such a hurry. She yanks me off the chair and pulls me into the second suffocating hug of the day. Seriously, I can barely breathe, and I'm super embarrassed with Kash and Barn in the room watching, but Mom isn't about to let go any time soon.

"You almost gave me two heart attacks in one day! How can you do this to your poor mother? Why do you get yourself into these situations, why?"

"I'm sorry, Mom." My voice comes out kind of muffled because she's crushing me against her. "The Sherlock thing came over me."

She pulls back and glowers with a fury I haven't seen in a long time. She's *really* mad this time. "You and the Sherlock thing! It's going to get you killed!"

I'm about to protest when suddenly Mom lets go and Kash pulls me into a hug. If you think I was humiliated being hugged by my mom, being hugged by my friend—who's also a girl—is a *thousand* times worse.

"I'm okay, Kash, really."

I gently push her away and adjust my wildly askew glasses.

Kash has a look on her face remarkably like the one my Mom wears. I guess females must perfect that look in order to reprimand guys who do crazy stuff that scares them.

Barn looks embarrassed for me – his mom excels at the guilt thing, too.

"He's fine, Abigail," Ari says, coming to my rescue, for which I'm grateful.

Still incensed, Mom turns on Ari like a rabid dog. "If you didn't fill his head with cases to investigate, none of this would've happened!"

"Mom!" I step around the desk to Ari's side. "He almost died trying to save me."

"And you wouldn't have needed saving if not for him!"

I've never seen Mom so furious.

Kash's mouth hangs open and Barn looks stunned.

"You can't talk to Ari that way!" My voice is shrill and angry and defiant. I am my mother's son.

Ari's strong hand lands on my trembling shoulder, his fingers gently squeezing in that calm way he has. "She's right, Mo."

I look at him, aghast. "No, she's not!" I turn back to Mom.

"You apologize to my Big Brother or I'll never talk to you again!"

I think I'm screaming now, but my brain has slid off the table into full ADHD mode and I'm not sure exactly *what* I'm doing.

Mom flinches and Kash gasps in horror.

"Mo!" That's Ari, but I keep my angry glare on Mom. "You don't talk to your mother that way."

Now I look over. "But she—"

He places his free hand on my other shoulder and squats down so we make eye contact. "What have I taught you about dealing with people, especially women?"

"To treat them with respect," I answer automatically because that lesson runs on auto-pilot. "But she had no right—"

He squeezes both shoulders this time, and I stop.

"Take deep breaths, Mo," he says, quietly and with assurance.

The look in his eyes borders on disappointment over my meltdown, and I *can't* disappoint him for anything! I breathe in deeply and let it out. I take more slow breaths while he gently massages my shoulders.

"Better?"

I nod and allow myself another few moments to calm down. The room is silent. The only sounds come from outside in the hall. I turn to Mom.

She's marveling, I know, at how quickly Ari can calm me down. He's better at it than she is, and maybe that's part of the problem. Maybe she's a little jealous of him?

"Mom, I love you, you know that," I say, keeping my voice steady, but making sure not to look at Barn or Kash. Mushy stuff like this is embarrassing at our age. "But I love Ari, too, and I *need* him."

Ari gasps ever so slightly, I guess because I've never told him I loved him before. Well, now he knows. And so does Mom.

She nods, like she's known this for years, and the anger on her face morphs into guilt.

"I know, sweetie." She gives Ari a sheepish look. "I'm sorry, Aristotle, for yelling at you. All the way over here I kept seeing my son dangling from that bird, not to mention careening down the street on his bike. I was just so scared."

"So was I," Ari admits, his voice sounding so heavy that I look over. He's eyeing me like I'm the most important thing he's ever seen. "I've never been so afraid in my life."

I hang my head because I really feel bad that I scared them. I guess for us kids it's easy to forget when we do something stupid that our folks freak out with worry.

"I'll be more careful," I say, making eye contact, first with Ari and then with Mom. "I promise."

I can see she's really ashamed for shouting at Ari that way. Even in the beginning, when she was still distrustful of a stranger taking out her little boy, she was never rude or disrespectful.

Taking on his detective role again, Ari stands and asks my friends if they want to add anything to my story.

"With Mo's memory? No way." That's Barn, tossing me a look of support.

Kash steps closer to Mom and there's some kind of fellowship between them, like I always see with girls at school.

"Thanks to Mo, we're still alive," she says, and my mouth drops open. "And thanks to Ari for teaching him how to stay calm. I was so scared I couldn't even think straight."

I'm stunned, because she was the one who brought me back when I sank into that funk over the "nosily yours" insult, but Mom looks equal parts relieved and remorseful. She glances at Ari and me.

"I guess my son is growing up, huh?"

Ari squeezes my shoulder. "He sure is."

There's a knock on the door and Ari says, "Come."

The door opens and an officer I recognize by sight, but not by name, enters carrying a phone.

"My phone!" I can't believe it.

The officer hands it to Ari and grins at me. "It's that indestructible case you put on. Good call, kid."

"My bike?" I'm sure I know the answer.

The officer frowns. "Totaled, I'm afraid." He leaves.

Ari clears his throat. "I was thinking you needed a

teenager bike anyway since you'll be one soon. We'll go shopping this weekend."

Yeah, I'll be thirteen in June.

"Thanks, Ari," I say, a bit uncertainly.

Becoming a teenager, especially when I'm so small and runty, is kind of scary.

Once again, Ari reads my mind. "That's when I got my first big growth spurt, when I turned thirteen."

I look up at his grinning face. "Yeah?"

"Yeah."

I smile and take the phone from him. The hard-shell cover is scuffed, but otherwise it's undamaged. I slip it into my pocket.

Mom says, "I think it's way past time to go home and relax. I feel like I've been chased by a chainsaw-wielding maniac and then flown around by a giant bird."

I look at her and she winks. When Mom is calm, she's pretty awesome, which is probably why she has so many subscribers to her channel.

I grin. "Yeah, I can imagine how tiring that must be."

She laughs and I know all is well again. At least until the next time I freak her out.

Media vans and reporters, surrounded by curious onlookers, are camped outside my house when we get home. Barn's mom and Kash's dad showed up at the station and took them home, so it's just Mom and me pulling into my driveway. I stare out the back window at the scads of media people with their cameras and microphones aimed my way.

"You go in the back, Mo," Mom says quietly. "I can talk to them."

As a famous YouTuber, Mom has done lots of interviews on local TV stations and even one on CNN. Unlike me, no one makes fun of her. She'd bite their head off.

I sigh heavily. At least that photo had my face blotted out, I'm thinking, so maybe it won't be so bad talking to the press. "I'll talk to them."

She places a strong hand on my shoulder. "If anyone laughs at you, they're toast." She smiles, but she's serious, too.

With Mom leading the way, I walk down the driveway to the gathered horde pooled on the sidewalk. Questions fly at me from every direction and my brain starts spinning. That's what happens with information overload.

"Muppit Boy! Muppit Boy! Over here, Muppit Boy!"

I look this way and that.

"Do you know why those people were after you?"

"Why did that bird save you?"

I try to open my mouth, but questions keep coming until my mother holds up her hand and, gradually, the reporters stop yelling. At least ten microphones point at my face, like guns about to blow me away.

"My son is unharmed and will answer a few of your questions," Mom says in her professional broadcaster voice. "Per order of the police department, he cannot reveal any sensitive information. This case is still fluid. Now, your questions."

The hands fly up like they do in my classroom when a teacher asks who wants to win a treat.

Mom points to a lady holding a Channel 4 microphone.

"Muppit Boy, why did that bird save you?"

I take a step forward, allowing my hair to stay swept across my face. "Uh, I don't know. It just showed up and grabbed me."

From the crowd, someone yells, "Probably saw your nose and thought you were a bird, too."

A few people chuckle and I burn with humiliation. Scanning the crowd, I spot Mason Rizzo lurking near the periphery.

Mom must've spotted him, too, because she starts forward, and I grab her hand. But that doesn't stop her mouth.

"I know you, Mason Rizzo, so you get out of here before I contact your parents!"

Rizzo laughs derisively. "They make fun of his nose, too," he shoots back with a chortle.

Mom gasps in shock. She spends so much time fielding

comments on YouTube that she isn't used the kind of in-your-face garbage I deal with every day.

Another reporter presses forward holding a photo in one hand and a Channel 7 mic in the other.

"Muppit Boy, are these the people who abducted you? What's happening in this photo?"

I gag. It's the picture Kash took, the one with my nose jutting out, the chainsaw at my throat, and the two maniacs on either side of me. How? Ari told the cops to blur my face!

"Where did you get that?" Mom ignores Rizzo for the moment and glowers at the reporter. She must look pretty scary because the man flinches back.

"It's all over the wire," he says, keeping his voice steady. "Cops are looking for these two. Are they the kidnappers, Muppit Boy?"

My spinning brain is getting worse, and I can't take this anymore.

"I am *not* Muppit Boy!" I don't realize that I'm screaming. "My name is Mo and that picture isn't funny!"

The reporter lowers the photo. "No one's saying this is funny."

"I think it is," Rizzo calls from in back. "Love the way your nose looks 3D!"

That's it! I lunge forward, fully intending to beat the snot out of Rizzo or die trying! Strong hands grip me from behind and yank me back.

"Mo!"

I struggle, knowing it's Mom. When I was younger, she was like a pro wrestler when these rages took over, and she knew just how to hold me so I didn't hurt her or anyone else. But once Ari came on the scene, Mom lost her touch. I'm pulling free when I hear a small child start bawling.

"Mommy, you said that was Muppit Boy!"

I freeze. The child wails with anguish and I turn to look over the crowd.

A woman I don't recognize holds a little girl who's maybe four. The girl is wailing and pointing at me with tears streaming from her eyes.

"It's okay, Millie, he's just being mean. Let's go home."

The mother glares at me and my brain shifts from fury mode to remorse mode, just like that.

"You said I could get Muppit Boy's autograph!" the girl screeches, and the mother pats her gently on the back in a soothing gesture that proves unsuccessful.

As they start to leave, I call out, "Wait!" and pull away from Mom.

"Mo!"

I ignore Mom and work my way through the now-silent crowd. I guess the screaming little girl got everyone's attention. I stop before them. The mother gives me the death stare, but I focus on the girl. What was her name? Oh, yeah.

"Millie, look at me."

The girl slowly turns her head, and my heart lurches at her devastated, tear-streaked expression.

"I'm sorry I shouted back there. I just got mad. Of course, I'm Muppit Boy. See?"

I sweep the hair from my face and offer her a three-quarters profile so she can clearly see my nose. Am I embarrassed in front of all these people? Beyond belief! But I'm beginning to understand that some things are more important than me—like not hurting little children.

The girl breaks into a smile so huge it fills up her face and she claps with gusto. "It is Muppit Boy, Mommy, it is!"

Now her mother smiles, too, and I turn back to the little girl.

She throws out her arms. "Can I hug you?"

I eye the mother, and she nods. I guess I'm forgiven for my meltdown. I reach for Millie and the girl practically leaps into my arms. Suddenly I'm holding her and she's hugging me like I'm a beloved teddy bear.

"Oh, Muppit Boy, you're my favorite character ever!"

Okay, another breach of Boy Code idiocy right here. I choke up and feel like crying, both for her and for how I almost destroyed her illusion. How on earth could Muppit Boy be so important to people? I hold her for a few moments and then set her down.

She takes my hand and grins, like I'm her best friend. "Can I get a picture with you?"

I smile and Millie presses up against me. Her mother holds out a phone and snaps a few photos before slipping the phone into her pocket. Millie leans in and kisses me on the cheek, sending another wave of awkwardness washing through me.

Millie's mother looks down at me and mouths, "Thank you."

I offer my best smile and then tousle Millie's hair before moving back through the crowd to my mom. It's like everyone was frozen in time because suddenly questions sail through the air again from all sides. Mom steps forward, but I wave her back. That moment with Millie has cleared my head and calmed me down. I hold up my hand for silence, and after a few moments, I get it.

"I can't tell you anything because I don't have the answers. I'm sure the police will know more once they catch the people who tried to hurt me and my friends." I pause and force my head to stay up so the cameras can see my eyes. "Having that chainsaw to my throat might look funny to some of you, but it wasn't to me. I could've died. As to the bird"—I toss a look out toward Rizzo, who stands there smirking—"it saved my life and gave me the chance to fly. Any kid out there who says they wouldn't wanna fly is lying. But I'm also happy the bird brought me back to earth."

Laughter wafts through the crowd and I'm momentarily stunned. I made people laugh without making a fool of myself?

"Anyway, that's all I have. Thanks for coming by." I wave and then turn down the driveway, heading for the back door.

Mom says, "Show's over," and then she's by my side.

We enter the yard and she pulls out her house key. As the door swings open and I start to enter, she touches my shoulder. I turn.

"I don't think I've ever been more proud of you."

It's Boy Code overload day! I choke up and tears blur my vision before I hurry into the house.

Mom follows and closes the door.

Chapter 9

Who Is This Dr. Drug?

Mom gets a call from St. Mary's informing her that the middle school will be meeting in the church until repairs to the school building can be completed. Seventh grade meets only from ten to noon, but there will be lots of homework to make up for the missing hours. Oh, joy.

I sit in front of my computer watching news coverage of my escapades, cringing with humiliation. Of course, the interview and everything with Millie has been shown over and over again, including when I turned my head to give Millie a clearer view of my nose. That part's bad, but the joy filling my soul at Millie's reaction makes it tolerable.

But people in the funeral procession, not to mention the news copter, got footage of me dangling like a helpless loser from the bird's claws and, worst of all, the copter captured the moment the bird leaned in to rub its beak against my nose! Many of the headlines on social media are geared toward making people laugh—at my expense, naturally.

A few of the worst are "Muppit Boy is Back – And This Time He Flies," "Muppit Boy Returns to Nose Around," "Muppit Boy Takes Flight," "Muppit Boy Meets His Match" (for the beak to nose shot), and "Great Noses Think Alike." And, of course, the chainsaw photo has been on every single news channel and all over the internet. On Facebook, I see "Muppit Boy" at the top of the Trending list and hundreds of comments about my adventures. Some of the comments are good and talk about me like I'm some kind of hero, but a lot of people are just into making fun of how goofy I look.

By the way, about that picture. Ari told me his captain wouldn't allow the photo to be altered because it was evidence. There wasn't time to blur my face since the suspects were still at large and the pic had to get out right away. He sounded so guilty, I felt bad for him.

"I let you down, Mo, and I hate doing that more than anything."

What could I say? It wasn't his fault. "It's okay, Ari. You tried."

He sounded morose when he hung up, but not as morose as I'm feeling right now as I search through news and internet channels. My attempt to stay off the radar by avoiding Mom's show backfired big time and Muppit Boy is once again the main attraction, at least the main *comic* attraction. I guess I might be paranoid, but there doesn't seem to be much attention paid to the fact that I could've died.

Most accounts treat the story like it was an episode of Mom's show, and some even suggest that everything that happened was faked to gain more followers. What I'm beginning to understand from scrolling through all the stories and comments is that many people seem to think *all* my embarrassing moments as a child were set up and staged by Mom to grow her YouTube following, and that's why people mock me so much, because they think it's all a phony, Reality TV-show act and I was in on the "joke." I guess people see so much fake stuff these days that they think everything is staged.

Oh, about the bird. I found out from the news that it's a rare California Condor and they aren't native to these parts. That information piques my Sherlock instincts. Why was that bird even in the area to rescue me?

It's seven o'clock when the doorbell rings upstairs. I hear Mom answer and then Ari's voice.

"Can I see Mo, Abigail?"

"Of course, Aristotle," Mom replies easily.

I leap from my computer chair and bolt for the stairs. Bounding into the front entry hall, I find Ari and Mom standing by the door.

I blurt, "Did you find anything out, Ari?"

Ari steps forward and claps me affectionately on one shoulder. "It's a bit involved, Mo. Could we go into the living room and talk, Abigail?"

"Of course, Aristotle," Mom says and ushers us past her. I see on her face that she still feels guilty for the way she yelled at Ari earlier.

We settle into the living room—Ari and me on the couch and Mom in her favorite kick-back chair.

"We believe the elderly couple who pursued you, Mo, work for a shadowy character who goes by the moniker, Dr. Drug," Ari says, mainly to me, but he makes sure to include a look toward Mom.

I sit bolt upright on the couch. "That's the guy they were gonna take me to!"

Ari nods. "That's why I'm here, just in case you can think of anything else you forgot earlier that might help us find him."

I give Ari one of my tilted head looks that screams '*Of course I didn't forget anything*'. "You know how my brain works, Ari. You got it all." Then I do remember something and turn to Mom. "I forgot to tell you, Mom. This Dr. Drug guy is a fan of your show."

She doesn't look pleased. "Lovely."

Ari leans forward and fixes me with an intense gaze. "Can you repeat everything you heard about the island and the rocket?"

I rewind my brain to that part of the incident. "The old lady said Dr. Drug wanted them on the island asap. The man asked about the missing hearing aids and the woman said Dr.

Drug told her not to worry about them now because the rocket was almost ready."

Mom listens intently until I finish. "The island must mean Catalina, don't you think, Aristotle?"

Ari nods. "I agree. We'll contact the Sheriff's department out there to begin a search."

"Who is this Dr. Drug?" I ask. "Did you find out more about him?"

"The FBI was helpful in that arena," Ari says. "He's an international black market pharmaceutical dealer and one of the richest men in the world. They don't know his true identity, but one of his most lucrative businesses is allergies."

"I don't understand," Mom replies, looking puzzled.

"Think back, Abigail, to elementary school. Did many children have peanut or gluten or other food allergies?"

Mom considers a moment. "Now that you mention it, no. And I never heard about such allergies on the news, but now it seems everyone has them."

"That's because they're relatively new," Ari goes on, sounding like one of my teachers. "Even bee sting allergies have risen substantially over the past ten years. Dr. Drug refined those allergies, found ways to infect larger portions of the populace than ever before, and now they're part of our genetic make-up."

Mom looks horrified. "But why would he do something so insidious?"

"Money. He has ties to all the major drug manufacturers

and profits off the antidotes to those allergic reactions. The FBI thinks hearing aids are a method Dr. Drug uses to ship microorganisms all over the world undetected."

I confess, I'm as shocked as my mom. "Then why were the old people looking for just one hearing aid?"

"That's a good question. They suspect the aid in question is a prototype, maybe a sample of some microorganism Drug doesn't want released just yet, but it somehow got distributed with a batch of other hearing aids he sent out."

"That's crazy," I mutter, mulling over everything Ari has just shared.

"It is," Ari agrees. "We're working with the FBI as well as other agencies. They all have that photo of the suspects, so it's only a matter of time before they are spotted."

I guess I make a tiny sound in my throat at the mention of the photo because Ari glances at me and I see guilt in his eyes.

"I thought you looked very brave in that picture, Mo," Mom says with quiet assurance. "Most people would have been too terrified to keep a clear head, but not you."

"I agree," Ari adds, one hand landing on my shoulder with a gentle squeeze.

My face feels hot, and I know I'm redder than a fire truck, but I also feel a stab of positive self-worth. I push the hair away from my eyes and look across at Mom. "Kash helped a lot."

"You have good friends, honey," she adds, and I silently agree.

I turn to Ari. "Did you find out anything about the condor that saved me?"

He shakes his head. "That's a mystery." Then he says to Mom, "I'd better go, Abigail. I'm point man on this case, and they need me at the station."

Mom offers a smile. "Thank you, Aristotle, for everything."

I know she means *everything* he's ever done for me, but I'm not sure Ari picks up on that.

Ari tousles my frizzy hair and smiles. "This is my boy right here." He winks and that draws a smile from me. Then he's gone, too, and it's just Mom and me.

There's a long moment of awkward silence.

I look up at her and shove my bangs aside. "What are your subscribers saying about me? Still mocking my nose?"

Her face shifts into a pained expression. "You know I block those people and always have. And I haven't posted any videos of you since you asked me not to."

I nod, thinking about Millie again. "You can post the video of me with Millie, if you want."

She looks surprised. "You sure? I mean, it does have that profile shot and all."

"I know, but it's okay." I pause. "I never knew Muppit Boy meant so much to people."

"He means the world to me." She has that look on her face and I know she needs a hug, so I reach out and wrap my arms around her.

My emotions feel more cluttered than my brain and I need to read some Sherlock Holmes stories. Those always redirect me so I can feel whole again.

I pull away from Mom. "I'm gonna go read for a while."

"Good idea."

I head down to my basement room and pull on some pajamas. Then I slip under the covers with *The Complete Sherlock Holmes* nestled lovingly on my stomach. I guess my body is more tired than I think because I barely get through one story before the world vanishes and I'm gone.

Chapter 10

We Just Want To Talk, Muppit Boy

The next day, I meet Barn and Kash at the corner, like always. "You guys okay?"

Barn nods because he's chewing something, most likely another breakfast bar.

Kash studies me. "Are *you* all right? I saw everything on the news last night."

"Yeah, I'm good."

We walk a moment in silence.

"I thought what you did for that little girl was the nicest thing ever."

I look over at Kash and see she's dead serious. "Uh, thanks."

"Anything new on the case?" Fortunately, Kash doesn't get all soppy like my mom, and her question puts me back on safer ground.

As we near St. Mary's, I fill them in on what Ari told me as the three of us head for the open double doors. I check out the school building and see police tape blocking the front entrance and wonder how much damage there was and how long it will take to repair.

The teachers are all aflutter when they see me and gush over how scared they were while watching the news and toss out a million questions at once.

One lady—Mrs. Miller—exclaims, "My daughter kept screaming, 'Muppit Boy's gonna get hurt, mommy' and she cried until she saw you were safe."

I smile tightly because other kids hear her. "I'm fine," I say, giving Mrs. Miller the evil eye for calling me that name.

She must get the message because her face crumbles. "Sorry, Mo. We were just so worried for you, my daughter and I."

"It's okay," I mumble.

Kash nudges me and I move into the shadowy interior of the church. Pews extend forward on either side of me all the way up to, and surrounding, the altar.

With Barn and Kash on either side of me, I walk up to where Mr. Hanson—our math teacher—is waving his arms like he's fighting off an invisible swarm of wasps.

"I think he wants us to sit up there," Barn says in his deadpan tone of voice.

Kash tilts her head. "You think so, huh?" The sarcasm could knock you over.

Barn, of course, doesn't catch it. "Yeah, I do. Look at how he's waving his arms and pointing to those pews."

Kash makes a disgusted sound under her breath.

Not wanting to call more attention to myself than just being here is already doing, I hurry to the indicated pew and brush past Mr. Hanson. Barn and Kash scoot in right after, and then some of our classmates. I glance around, making sure not to make eye contact with anyone, but search for Rizzo. Fortunately, he and his cronies are across the aisle and two pews up. That means no spitballs in the back of my head. From them, anyway.

From what Mom told me, each of my six teachers will get twenty minutes to present a lesson and give us homework for the next day, and that's how everything unfolds.

When it's Sister Ella's turn to teach science, she turns to write something on a mobile whiteboard, and I hear a sharp whisper from two pews up.

"Hey, Muppit Boy!"

I glance in that direction and see a kid who excels at mocking my nose. I grimace, but he's pointing across the aisle, so I look in that direction. I freeze.

Rizzo wears a gigantic nose made from folded binder paper. He's holding it in place while rubbing the tip against Mazza's nose, clearly imitating me and the condor and drawing titters from everyone around him. I feel my face flame red and look down at my shoes. Kash mutters something impolite under her breath about what she's going to do to Rizzo after school.

I'm about to lean in and tell her to ignore it when Sister Ella says, "I'll take that, Mason."

I look up. She's standing in the aisle, her arm extended toward Rizzo, palm open. Having lost the smirk, Rizzo reluctantly hands over the paper nose.

"You two will stay after school."

Rizzo groans and glares at me, like it's *my* fault he's such a dirtbag. I'm slightly heartened to hear laughter from my peers because it's directed at Rizzo, not me.

Sister Ella returns to the whiteboard and tosses the crumpled nose into a wastebasket before instructing us to copy down the homework assignment. I'm about to start copying when I feel eyes on me and turn quickly, expecting to be hit with a spitball.

It's Miriam Munson (which doesn't preclude a spitball, but she's more the instigator type) staring at me. She extends her right hand, offering me a folded piece of paper.

Reluctantly, not wanting to call attention to myself, I snatch the paper and turn back around. I'm supposed to be copying the assignment, but I'm curious and unfold the paper. Scrawled in neat cursive is '*I thought the picture of you and the bird was cute*'.

Huh? I'm about to turn around when the note is snatched from my hand by Kash. She reads it and her face turns stormy. She scowls at me before looking over her shoulder. I note Miriam's eyes widening with fear, and when I glance at Kash I understand why. If looks could kill, the whole church would be dead.

Kash crumples up the paper and whispers in my ear, "Did you forget Valentine's Day already?"

I stiffen with shame. I guess humiliations are such a daily occurrence, I force myself to never replay them. This past Valentine's Day, us kids handed out cards to each other, but of course I didn't get any except from Kash and Barn. What can I say? Charlie Brown has nothing on Muppit Boy.

Anyway, Miriam comes up to me as I'm entering the cafeteria for lunch and hands me a card. I'm stunned because, well, like what I said about Charlie Brown. I open the card with caution, expecting it to blow up in my face. It doesn't. There's a cute bear on it—yeah, the bear has a big nose, but I ignore that because it's the first card I can remember getting. I don't even know what to say since she's never been nice to me before, so I mumble, "Thank you," and turn to leave.

As I turn, I realize too late that Miriam's friend, Liliana, is holding up a small carton of milk and it's right at the level of my face. Naturally, as they'd planned, my nose strikes the milk and knocks it out of her hand. It slams to the floor and white liquid splashes my dark corduroy pants and soaks my shoes and socks.

Both girls sink into gales of laughter and that's when I notice their other friend, Wendy, filming everything on her phone. I remember my eyes burning with potential tears.

While I might not care about the Boy Code with Ari, I sure as heck do with mean girls like these. I throw the Valentine card onto the cafeteria floor and run out the door, away from their derisive laughter.

Just replaying the scene makes me bristle with anger. "Thanks, Kash."

She shoves the crumpled note into her backpack, and we write down the assignment.

The moment our teachers dismiss us at noon, Sister Ella's melodic voice calls out, "Mason and Lorenzo, up front, please."

I note from the corner of my eye that Rizzo is glowering at me, but I pretend to be tightening the straps on my backpack and don't look his way. Once we're outside, I search for Miriam to make sure she's not trying to pull another stunt—the video of my nose spilling the milk went viral, by the way—but I don't see her.

Both Kash and Barn insist they need to go *straight home* or their parents will call Ari. Yeah, having a Big Brother who's a cop is cool—*most* of the time. I'd like to do more detective work, but I really don't have any clues to follow up on, so we all head home.

I'm feeling restless after an hour and a half of homework and really need to get outside. With the chainsaw maniacs—as Mom calls them—still at large, I know she won't let me go out without her. But I don't want to talk to anyone right now, so I decide to sneak out for a short walk and leave my phone in my room. I know that part's risky if anything happens to me, but Mom always has my phone on the tracker app and she'll for sure be checking it every five minutes after yesterday, even though she thinks I'm downstairs. Since I won't be gone long, it seems like an acceptable risk.

I wait till I hear her going into the bathroom and then I tiptoe up the stairs and out the back door. I stick to the quiet alleys between houses, hoping to avoid other people. To calm my spirits, I wear my ear buds and crank the audiobook version of *The Adventures of Sherlock Holmes* from my old mp3 player. Okay, not cool, I know, but rap music just makes my brain go crazy and I can't stand classical stuff. Boring!

Anyway, I'm chilling as I walk, hood up, totally engrossed in the story, when suddenly I catch movement at the corner of my eye. I whirl around just in time to confront a big man wearing a dark suit lurking directly behind me. I spin around to run, but there's an even bigger man in black blocking the way ahead. I glance to my left and there's a black car with the back door open. I was so caught up in the audiobook, I didn't even hear it approach! I turn back to the guy in front of me. He taps his ear and I realize he's telling me to remove the ear buds. I pull them out, my heart pounding with dread. These are the same guys I saw the other day at school, at least this one. He's the one who stared at me from the car window.

"We just want to talk, Muppit Boy," comes a male voice from inside the car.

I don't approach but do lean down to peer into the shadowy interior.

A third man in black, wearing sunglasses and going bald, from what I can see, reclines casually against the rear seat.

"Who are you?"

"I work with the condor, the one that rescued you yesterday."

I confess, that's not the response I expected. "You work with a bird?"

"Charlie is no ordinary bird, and you are no ordinary boy. We need to talk." He reaches into his jacket pocket, and I flinch back, but he only extracts an official-looking ID.

I lean in to see the badge he holds out. Homeland Security. Ari was right! My brain tells me to run, but the Sherlock part screams, '*This is the chance you've been waiting for*!'

"How long will it take?"

"Not long," the man replies, but offers no specific details.

"I need to let my Big Brother know I'm going with you."

"You may text Detective Galanos from one of our secure phones. He won't be able to trace the text, of course, but he'll know you are safe. And he will be able to send texts to you."

"How do you know about Ari?"

"We know everything about you, Muppit Boy. In fact, I'm

something of a fan." He laughs to himself. "My favorite episode is the one—"

"It's okay, you don't have to tell me," I interrupt because I just can't relive another humiliating moment from my childhood.

I hesitate. Getting into a car with strangers, especially the kind who look like they could toss NFL players around, doesn't seem like a good idea. But then I think of what's been going on and how I might be able to learn something important.

"Okay."

I cautiously slide into the backseat and my door is closed by one of the big guys. Then they take over the driver and shotgun seats. I gaze at the man across from me and notice that he's staring at my face.

"I've grown, that's why it looks bigger."

"I wasn't staring at your nose. I was just thinking how my daughter will be jealous that I met you."

My mouth drops open in shock, but his unchanged facial expression tells me he's serious. "Oh."

We stop talking as the car picks up speed and rounds a corner. The back windows are so heavily tinted from the inside that I can't see out, and there's a barrier that slides into place between the front seats and back, so I can't see anything in that direction, either.

I guess they don't want me to know where we're going.

That's probably not good.

Chapter 11

Put On The Guy Who Grabbed You

I exchange a few texts with Ari on the way and—needless to say—he goes ballistic when I tell him where I am and who I'm with. He demands to hear my voice on the phone. I look over at Mr. Silverman—that's the guy in back with me—and relay the message.

Silverman lets out a heavy sigh. "Even law enforcement doesn't trust the government." He taps a button on his phone and hands it back.

Ari's frantic face fills the screen. "Mo! Thank God!"

"Ari, I'm fine."

Ari looks angry. "Put on the guy who grabbed you."

"He didn't grab me, Ari," I say. I've already texted him this assurance, but I guess he's scared. "I got in the car on my own."

He opens his mouth to speak, and I suspect it will be

something uncomplimentary about me thinking like a little kid, but he pauses. "Put him on."

I hand the phone to Silverman. He takes it in his right hand, and I notice he wears a gold ring, and his fingers are long and slender.

"Detective Galanos, this is Oscar Silverman."

"What do you want with my boy?" Ari's voice pounds through the phone speaker like a cannon shot.

Silverman holds the phone at arm's length. "We need him to rewind his brain and tell us everything he told you."

There's a pause and then Ari says, "How do you know about his rewind trick?"

"Detective, we find out what we need to know, and right now the information in his head could prevent a major catastrophe."

"What are you talking about?"

I'm leaning in because I want to know, too.

"Our intel suggests Dr. Drug is planning something that could infect millions of Americans and that he will launch his attack sometime in the next twenty-four to forty-eight hours. It is our hope Muppit Boy has information in his head that might have seemed insignificant to you but will give us the clue we need to stop that event from occurring."

"His name is Mo, not Muppit Boy!" Ari snaps.

I lean closer so he can see me. "It's okay, Ari. He didn't mean anything by it. If I can help stop Dr. Drug, I want to."

Ari frowns and looks scared, and he *really* hates being scared. "I should be there with you."

"Detective," Silverman says, "we will let you know when and where we plan to drop off your boy so you can meet him. Will that be equitable?"

Ari isn't happy, but what choice does he have? "It's not great, but it's a plan." He looks around. "Mo?"

I lean in and Silverman tilts the phone.

"You be careful."

"I will." I offer a smile, even pushing the hair off my face so he can see I'm not afraid.

The call ends and Silverman pockets his phone. "That call was encrypted, by the way, in case your Big Brother has any plans to trace it."

I nod because I'm sure that's exactly what Ari's trying to do.

Mr. Silverman doesn't ask me any questions and we ride in silence for a few minutes. Then we turn left and drop down a steep incline. The sudden change in angle makes me glad I'm wearing a seatbelt.

"Your headquarters are underground?"

Silverman peers at me. "We might just be descending into an underground garage."

I pause to consider that, listening intently for sounds outside the car.

"I don't think so. I don't hear any car sounds, but I do hear water lapping against something. I think we're underground somewhere near the harbor or the beach."

A tiny smile breaks Silverman's stoic expression. "Very good, Muppit Boy."

The car makes more turns, always descending lower, and I ask, "How many floors below ground will we go?"

"Can you tell?"

The car begins to slow as it levels out. I rewind my brain to the moment we started downward and replay each turn of the car. I think each turn leads to another level, like in above-ground parking structures.

"Five," I announce as the "tape" comes to an end.

He looks impressed. "You're quite gifted. I look forward to getting to know you better."

My door is pulled open by one of the agents while Silverman exits on his side of the car. We are in a large parking garage and there are several elevators just ahead bearing the Homeland Security Seal.

Silverman ushers me toward one of the elevators and I head in that direction. I'm flanked by the two burly agents, who act like I'm gonna try to escape and they look ready to jump me at a moment's notice. Silverman's heels click on the pavement behind me, but I'm afraid to look back. I really don't want to spook the big guys. I bet they could body slam Godzilla.

The guy on my right presses the "Up" button and the

elevator doors swoosh open. I step inside the cramped interior and stand in back. The two agents crowd together in front of me as Silverman joins us.

I'm not even sure I should share this next embarrassment but, oh, well, here goes. The men back up so close that my nose presses into one of their backs and I have to turn my head to the side to be comfortable. Okay, 'nuff said about the elevator ride.

My heart pounds with excitement at the possibility of seeing a real secret government lab and headquarters, but when the elevator doors slide open, I find myself on an ordinary-looking office building floor with plain wooden doors. My hopes further plummet when Silverman ushers me into an office with a big desk and some chairs. There are nature landscapes on the walls and several photos of people I presume are his family.

He moves around the large wooden desk and indicates a plush-looking chair in front of it. But my gaze hasn't left those family photos. I practically hold my breath as I take two steps closer and lean in to examine one of them. It depicts a young girl, maybe five or six, clutching a toy to her heart and grinning broadly for the camera. To my horror, it's a Muppit Boy doll!

Okay, I better explain. When I was five, my mother dressed me up in a larger version of the furry red onesie, took pictures, and then made a deal with a toy manufacturer to sell Muppit Boy dolls that were basically a boy—me, big nose included—wearing the furry red onesie. And they sold like tickets to a preview screening of the next *Star Wars* movie. Mom made sure all the proceeds went to help children with cancer and many people loved the idea so much they bought a doll for every kid they knew, even ones who never watched the show. And Mom ended up with tons more followers who wanted to see the "real" Muppit Boy in action.

Needless to say, as I got older, I was horrified to see kids with those dolls, especially when they recognized me by my most prominent feature. After I turned ten, I begged my mom to stop the company from making any more dolls, and since her contract was about to expire, she agreed. Seeing Silverman's daughter holding "me" brings back conflicted memories.

"I told you my daughter was a fan," I hear from behind.

I whirl around, having almost forgotten the man was there.

He stands behind his desk studying me in that analytical way he has. "That was her favorite toy for a long time. She rubbed the fur off that one and I tried to buy another, but was surprised to hear the manufacturer had ceased making them."

I blush and glance down.

"I thought it odd at the time," Silverman goes on, still gazing at me with such force that I don't want to look up. "I know they sold well and raised a great deal of money for cancer research."

Suddenly, stopping those dolls because they embarrassed

me doesn't sound like such a great idea. I never asked Mom how much money went to the kids with cancer. Maybe I should have.

"Sit down, Mo, and let's talk. We're on a timeline here."

I nod, without looking up, and move to the plush chair. I lower myself into it and marvel at the softness of the leather. I hear Silverman settle into his own chair because it creaks as he shifts position.

"As I said in the car," he continues, "I need you to rewind your brain, as you call it, and tell me everything about your experience at the school and when you were held against your will."

I still can't get the Muppit Boy dolls out of my mind. Was I selfish to stop them, or was Mom wrong for marketing them in the first place? Or maybe a combination of both?

"If you don't mind, I'd like to record your recitation."

I glance up, surprised. "Why?"

He offers a tight smile. "I don't have your video recorder memory, I'm afraid. As I told you, even the smallest detail might help us locate Dr. Drug and I don't want to miss anything while taking notes."

That makes sense. "Okay."

He opens the top drawer and pulls out a small pocket tape recorder.

I rewind my brain to yesterday morning when everything began and launch into a detail-by-detail account of all that happened.

Silverman listens with intense interest, occasionally jotting down a few notes, but mostly keeping his piercing gaze fixed on me like a laser beam.

"You're certain the woman said 'rocket'?" he asks when I finish.

"Yes, sir. Does that mean Dr. Drug plans to seed the atmosphere with some microorganisms he's created?" I'm not sure where that insight comes from, but there it is.

Silverman looks surprised. "An excellent deduction, Mo. Any other thoughts you'd like to share?"

I consider a moment. "Well, I've been thinking a lot about how she said Dr. Drug needed them out at the island and, well, around here anyone who says, 'the island' means Catalina."

He leans forward and clasps both hands on the desk. "You're certain? It couldn't be one of the other Channel Islands?"

"I don't think so. Catalina is the one everybody goes to. I've been there a few times on field trips. Maybe your men should check it out."

He hesitates, as though weighing a heavy decision, and then says, "We have. No trace of Dr. Drug or any suspicious activity."

My excitement dims somewhat, though I still believe Catalina is the right place. Could Drug have built something under the water nearby? As I reflect on everything I just shared with Silverman, I get another insight. "You guys control the super slug that attacked my school, don't you?"

Now he sits all the way back in his chair, eyes wide with amusement. "And the condor, as I mentioned in the car. His rescue of you, however, was unplanned."

I'm *more* confused, not less, but I try to think like Sherlock and ask the most logical question. "If he wasn't supposed to rescue me, why did he?"

"Our best guess is that he's a fan."

"Huh?"

Silverman appears even more perplexed as he leans forward again and studies me like I'm a science exhibit.

"Charlie—that's the name we gave him—seemed fascinated by your show while he recuperated from his surgery. Dr. Bell enjoys watching the older episodes online, and Charlie became oddly addicted to them. We sent him out yesterday to search for the old couple, who are known associates of Dr. Drug, because we had intel they'd been spotted in San Pedro. Both Bell and I are mystified as to how Charlie recognized you while doing reconnaissance, let alone why he would want to help you. But he apparently likes Muppit Boy, inasmuch as a condor can like anything, I suppose."

Great. Now I have bird fans.

But at least this bird saved your life.

I guess I'm so used to being mocked that I think all my fans are bad. Maybe that's my middle school brain at work.

"Can I see Charlie?"

Suddenly, I'm excited about seeing my rescuer again. That gentle moment where we brushed noses warms my heart every time I *don't* remember people laughing at it. I've never had a pet or been close to any animal, so it's a new experience for me.

Silverman considers the idea. "Bell and I talked about the possibility. Charlie is classified, as is everything we do here, and you are a civilian. Not to mention a child."

My mind rewinds to his earlier words. "But you said I'm no ordinary boy."

He smiles. "That brain of yours will teach me to take more care with my words." He hesitates. "Charlie has been agitated since his return. Bell thinks you might be able to calm him."

"So, I can see him?"

"If I allow this, I require your word that you will tell no one how Charlie is different. You may talk about Charlie, since they already know of him, but nothing more."

My face falls. "I can't even tell Ari?"

Silverman considers the request. "Him, I will allow. So long as he keeps the information confidential."

"He will. I tell him all kinds of things he never tells my mom about."

His eyebrows raise. "Indeed?"

I wait, gripping the arms of the chair, hoping he'll say yes.

Finally, like a balloon bursting, he stands and moves around the desk, towering over me. “Come with me.”

I leap from the chair, my brain threatening to derail from anticipation. Silverman opens the office door and ushers me out. I step into the bland corridor with its white walls and brown carpeting and Silverman leads me back to the elevators. This time, fortunately, there’s only the two of us in the tiny cubicle, so my nose is safe.

Chapter 12

Muppit Boy Could Be Killed

We descend two floors before the elevator stops and the doors slide open with barely a whisper. Silverman steps out and I follow him. This corridor sends my brain in every direction at once. It's clearly a science section with laboratories behind glass windows. I spot men and women in white coats engaged with computers, microscopes, machines I couldn't identify if I tried, and who knows what all else. I want to ask a thousand questions, but I don't want Silverman to think I'm being nosey. Okay, poor choice of words.

We stop before a thick glass door that has both a keypad and fingerprint reader. Silverman punches in a code he thinks I can't see but being short has its advantages and I read the numbers from under his raised arm. Then he presses his right index fingertip onto the small scanner. With a short *beep*, the door slides open.

We enter a high-tech lab bustling with people working at keyboards, studying data on video monitors, and running tests on equipment that looks like it belongs in a science fiction movie. The machines make weird sounds, there are muted conversations, and the clacking of fingers against computer keys fills the air.

My ADHD shifts into overdrive.

"Please keep your eyes on the floor as we walk through here, Mo," Silverman says, and I force myself to focus on him. "I don't want your brain recording any classified data."

I do what he says. Much as I want to look around, there's just too much activity all at once and I need to keep my brain on the table right now. I keep my gaze fixed on the back of Silverman's dress shoes as he leads the way through the lab. I hear a door opening with a buzzing sound and then I'm inside a large, expansive room with almost no equipment. Silverman closes the door behind me, cutting off the din.

My brain slides back into place in the quiet of this chamber and I look around. It feels like I'm inside a combination athletic training center and airplane hangar. It's long and cavernously high, likely taking up a huge portion of this entire facility. There are treadmills and metal weights of different styles, even kettlebells. I know what those are because Ari's taken me to the gym a few times and shown me how to work out.

There's only one man in this room, planted before a computer monitor typing something on the keyboard. He's bald on top with gray hair frizzing out along the sides and back. He wears a white smock, and his back is to us as we approach. I notice one of the treadmills running at a high speed, but no one's on it. I'm about to ask Mr. Silverman about this when he says, "Rudy."

The man spins in his swivel chair and I stifle a laugh. His eyebrows are so bushy they stick out at all angles, and his nose —I know, the pot calling the kettle, as Mom would say—seriously looks like a mushroom that somebody stepped on. And his face is flushed red, like he just ran ten miles on the treadmill. He has a thick gray mustache and worry lines around his eyes. But he smiles when he sees me.

"Muppit Boy!"

Ok, my nickname brings me back to earth. I guess he's not so funny-looking after all.

"Uh, hi."

He stands up and checks his readouts, completely ignoring us.

"Sir, your treadmill is on."

He turns around and I point at the moving treadmill ten feet away.

"Of course, it is," he replies, his voice deep and full, which surprises me. This guy could be an audiobook narrator with that voice. "I'm testing Sammy's speed."

Mystified, I look over at the treadmill. I'm about to say

again that no one's on it when something on the spinning belt catches my eye. It's small and dark and moving very fast. Without even thinking, I head in that direction, my gaze pinned to that tiny moving...something. I take five more steps, brushing the hair fully off my face, and freeze.

It's the slug! And it's running on a treadmill!

"Meet Sammy," I hear from behind me, but I can't pull my gaze from that thick, dark shape zipping along so fast I can barely make out any details. "Derisively dubbed by the pinheads at the Pentagon as the world's first Bionic Slug. Better, stronger, slimier."

I turn to the man in the white coat. "Seriously? You made a bionic slug?" The words are out before I can stop them. "Why not a dog or a horse or something useful?"

Surprisingly, he doesn't look offended. "Budget cuts." Then he giggles. "And you talk just like you do on the show. I love that sarcastic attitude you always take with your mother."

Okay, that shuts me up long enough for Silverman to step forward. His face remains deadpan, as usual. "Mo, meet Dr. Rudy Bell, our resident scientific genius."

Bell sticks out a finely manicured hand and we shake. For an old guy, his grip is firm.

"Pleasure to meet my grandson's favorite character."

I want to tell him I'm a real person, not a character, but my brain is spinning again with all this new information. A *beep* echoes through the room and the treadmill begins to slow. Bell excitedly scurries to the computer monitor while I focus on the slug gradually slowing down as the belt crawls to a stop. The slug looks just as ugly as it did in that alley, but it's also sweating now and that makes it even shinier. Do slugs sweat? I guess so.

"Ha!" Bell shouts behind me. "Sixty-three point four miles per hour. His best time ever!"

"Congratulations, Rudy," Silverman says, though he doesn't sound excited or even interested. "But we're here about Charlie."

Hearing his name, I scoot up to the two men.

"Is Charlie bionic, too?" My brain just connected those dots, and it would explain a lot.

"Not bionic," Bell says. "That's too old school, as you kids like to say. Charlie and Sammy are *nanonic*."

I must make a funny face because Bell claps like an excited child. "I remember that facial expression in the episode where your nose got caught in your mother's hairnet and yanked it off." He laughs. "Those were good times with my grandson."

I'm sure I've turned red again—it happens so often these days I think it's my permanent color now. "Not good for me," I mutter, but force my brain to stay on track. "So, what's nanonics?"

Bell opens his mouth to speak, but Silverman raises a hand. "Just the basics, Rudy. Classified, remember."

"Of course, of course."

He notes Sammy sliming his way down off the treadmill

to the floor and moves in that direction. I follow. To my utter disgust, Bell picks the slug off the floor and rests it on his palm. It's easily as long as his hand.

As he gently strokes the slimy black skin, Bell says to me, "You've heard of nanites, I presume?"

I roll my eyes. Hey, I'm twelve. "Look at this face. Am I a nerd?"

Bell chuckles. "Love the Muppit Boy sarcasm. Anyway, nanonics places microscopic nanites throughout the body and brain of an animal that enhance every aspect of the animal. Each nanite coordinates with all the others, like a beehive, and they're powered by tiny nuclear batteries that can last a hundred years."

My brain is processing all this data, but my gaze remains on the slug, and I keep hearing Barn say, "I wonder what slug dump feels like when it hits you." I decide not to find out for myself.

"What can Sammy do, besides move fast and break through walls?"

Bell's face takes on a look of pride. "He's the best drug-sniffing slug in the business." Then he shrugs. "Of course, he's the *only* drug sniffing slug in the business. But he's superb. That's what he was doing at the school. He detected something and went inside to find it."

I turn to Silverman. "He was looking for the missing hearing aid. You guys think there's some kind of drug hidden in it, don't you?"

Silverman's eyebrows shoot up. "As a matter of fact, we do. But Sammy didn't find anything."

"Did he have to destroy my school while he was looking?"

Bell looks embarrassed. "Sammy is a bit head-strong, as you discovered in the alley. He hasn't yet mastered self-control."

I think about how he should spend some time with Ari, but I don't say it.

"The old people didn't find it, either."

Silverman nods. "You mentioned that during your rewind."

Then another revelation hits me. "They're nanonic, too, aren't they? That's why they were so strong and fast."

Silverman looks surprised once again and hesitates before answering.

"Come on, you can tell me," I plead. "We're on the same side, right?"

Silverman pauses a moment. "We suspect Dr. Drug developed his own nanonic technology."

"We're not allowed to test ours on humans," Bell offers, sounding petulant. "Not till the FDA gives its approval and the red tape for that process takes years."

"FDA?"

"Food and Drug Administration," Bell replies. "Big government bureaucracy."

My brain is on overload again. Too much going on and

too many questions buzzing through my head. I need to shift to something concrete.

"What about Charlie?"

Bell beams with pride as he sets Sammy down atop the counter, beside his computer. The slug just sits there and looks, well, disgusting.

"Charlie represents some of my best work," Bell says as he faces me. "He came to us heavily damaged, his wings shredded, practically dead. My nanites saved his life. In addition, we used cartilage and feathers from other deceased birds to rebuild his wings—which is why he's multi-colored. The nanites healed his body and enhanced his strength five-fold." He fixes his wild, animated eyes on me. "When he swooped in and lifted you off that bike, *oooh,* was I excited!" He rubs his hands together like a witch concocting a potion. "You, Muppit Boy, awakened something in him that we needed."

Okay, my brain is gonna explode. "Uh, what?" I fight to keep my focus on his face.

"He's never cared for us," Bell goes on, his voice becoming staccato with his increased excitement. "He'd do what we wanted because we figured out how to communicate with his brain via computer. But you, Muppit Boy, he loves you!" He wrings his hands again. "This is the best *boy and his bird* story ever!"

I wanna say that it's probably the *only* boy and his bird story ever, but my brain is about to short-circuit. "Can I see Charlie now?"

"That's why we're here," Silverman intones.

I notice from the corner of my eye something in his hand. A remote maybe? It looks like he presses a button and then the wall at the far end of this chamber—which is the size of a football field, I'd say—slides up from the floor. A *squawk squawk* comes from the other side, and then with a flourish of wings that look like those of a small airplane, Charlie swoops into the room at a rapid speed. He aims straight for me.

"Charlie!" I call out with excitement as I step forward to greet him.

I catch movement and spot Bell skittering for the computer console.

"Wait!" barks Silverman.

"But Muppit Boy could be killed if I don't slow Charlie down," Bell says with urgency.

"Wait," Silverman repeats, but less sharply this time.

I only catch this exchange from the corner of my eye because I'm watching the massive condor bearing down on me like a missile. But I'm not afraid. Just when I think that razor sharp beak will rip through my head, Charlie flaps those ten-foot wings, blowing my hood back and my hair every which way as he settles lightly to the floor at my feet and folds the wings against his side more smoothly than I can slip into a tee shirt.

I drop to my knees, ecstatic to see this mangy-looking bird with the rainbow feathers. He emits a *squawk* that sounds happy and then his beak is rubbing against my nose. It tickles and my heart swells with a kind of joy I've never felt before, even with Ari. I guess my nose, and those embarrassing videos, have made me self-conscious around other people because I always feel like I can't measure up. But this animal, this bird most people would call ugly, *likes* me, maybe even *loves* me, just as I am. I rub my nose against that hard beak and grin with delight.

I'm vaguely aware of the two men speaking behind me.

"That was risky, Oscar."

"Maybe. But now we know Charlie can control his movements with precision, if he has a good reason to do so."

"And Muppit Boy gives him that reason."

"Exactly."

Charlie pulls his beak away and emits another *squawk*. Careful not to hit me, he spreads his wings and rises into the air, soaring back in the direction he came.

"Hey, Charlie, where you going?"

I watch him disappear through the large opening and feel a deep sense of loss. But then he swoops back into the chamber in a flourish of wings, carrying something in his mouth. This time he doesn't land, but majestically glides over my head and drops the "something." As it falls, I see it's a rubber ball, the kind that can bounce pretty high if you throw it hard. I reach out and grab the ball before it hits the floor. Charlie *squawks* from way down the chamber, circling high in the air. He's waiting.

My brain overflows with excitement. I turn to the two men. "Can I play with him?"

"Of course," says Silverman.

I throw the ball as hard as I can at one of the walls. I don't have a good throwing arm, but like I said, these balls do all the work for you. It strikes the wall and ricochets up toward the ceiling. Charlie streaks forward, a bullet with wings, and snatches it from the air before it can bounce somewhere else.

I applaud vigorously. "Way to go, Charlie!"

The bird acknowledges the compliment by doing a barrel roll on his way back to me. Once again, the ball drops, but this time it's like he aimed it perfectly because it drops right into my hands. I don't wait for him to get all the way down the chamber. I throw the ball as hard as I can. My shoulder screams from the effort, but I'm rewarded with a high arc that sails well over Charlie and out across the open space.

Charlie homes in on the ball at an astonishing speed as it drops back toward the floor. He swoops in a downward arc so fast I'm sure he'll hit the floor. But at the last second, he banks upward and clamps onto the ball with his beak and soars over to me. My heart wants to burst, and my brain is exploding like the finale of a fireworks show. I've never felt such a singular moment of pure happiness as I do right now.

I lose track of time as I try different ways to trick him with my throws. But he must sense where the ball will go because he's always right there snatching it out of the air. And then he does something different. On my last throw, he lets the ball bounce off the wall and then the floor and then another wall and then...he ignores it. Instead, he flies back and circles overhead, squawking and swooping close to me. I don't know what he wants.

"I think he's trying to tell you something," Bell says from behind me.

I whirl around. I'm sweating by now and my heart pounds from exertion. "Yeah?"

"Let me check the computer."

He hurries to the screen while I watch my new friend circle overhead. The ceiling is maybe twenty-five feet high, but the overall chamber is so expansive he has no trouble banking wide turns.

"This is quite unexpected, Oscar," Bell says. "Look what Charlie is saying."

Silverman strides to the computer console and gazes intently at the screen. He makes an odd exclamation of surprise, something between a grunt and a cough.

"What's he saying? You can read his words in there?" My brain is spinning again because I'm so hyped.

Bell studies me. "The nanites in Charlie's brain are linked to this computer. Over time, we've learned to interpret the meaning of his squawking sounds and have programmed the computer to respond. In fact, the nanites themselves allow Charlie to vocalize. Normally, condors make no sounds at all."

My breathing is still ragged from all that throwing, but I'm too excited to care. "What's he saying?"

"He's saying 'fly Muppit Boy'. I believe he wants to take you for a ride."

"Yes!"

Unlike yesterday, I have no fear at the prospect of Charlie flying me around. I hurry to a spot under him and stick my arms out to the sides so he can grab me under my armpits like before.

Charlie obviously gets the message because he swoops rapidly down, swinging around behind me. The next thing I know his huge claws grip my upper arms and then my heart isn't the only thing that's soaring. My stomach drops like I'm on a roller coaster at Six Flags and I'm up and away, flying around the chamber with Charlie's flapping wings pumping wind into my face and joy into my soul.

Charlie dips and rises and glides. I laugh and whoop and have the time of my life. My dangling legs swish back and forth like a pendulum and a couple of times Charlie swoops so low at Silverman and Bell that the men need to duck to avoid being kicked in the face. That makes me laugh all the harder.

I don't know how long we fly, but all too soon it's over and Charlie lowers me gently to the floor and releases his tight grip around my arms before swooping up and around to settle beside me. My arms and shoulders ache, and my ab muscles hurt from all the laughing, but my entire being swells with pure elation. I have to fight to keep my brain from slipping away completely.

"Thanks, Charlie," I gush. "That was the best!"

Charlie lets out a short *squawk* and then leans toward me. I drop to my knees at once and we rub noses. I seriously could stay this way forever, but a hand on my shoulder pulls me from my joy.

"I'd better get you back, Mo. We've been here longer than expected and I don't want to anger your Big Brother."

I lean away from Charlie and turn to see Silverman gazing down at me. "Do I have to leave?" I know I do, but I don't want to. "I want to play with Charlie some more." I'm still on my knees and must look like I'm begging.

"It would seem you will have other chances to play with Charlie."

"Really? I can come back?"

Bell strides over to stand beside Silverman and says, "I don't think Charlie will let us *not* bring you back. I doubt he'll cooperate ever again unless he can see you. I confess, I'm mystified. I've never heard of a bird showing such affection for a human, but maybe his nanite-infused brain has evolved to something resembling that of a dog. It will require further research."

My brain is recording, but I'm not listening. I just want a "yes" answer. "So that means I can come back?"

"It means you can come back," Silverman answers, his stoic face revealing what could pass for a smile.

I turn to Charlie. "You hear that, Charlie? I can come back!"

This time I lean in and rub my nose against his beak. He makes a low, almost purring sound, and I know he's happy. We remain like that for a few moments while I fight back tears. Even though we'll be together again, a terrible sense of loss washes over me. But I know I must go, so I finally stand.

"I'll be back soon, Charlie, so don't worry. You're my friend for life!"

I doubt Charlie understood a word I said, but he *squawks* with delight and flaps his wings a few times, drawing a hearty laugh from deep within me. And then I'm led out of the chamber, tossing one last wave at Charlie and feeling my excitement dim as the door closes and cuts him off from view.

Bell extends a hand. "It's been a pleasure, Muppit Boy. I expect we'll be seeing a lot more of you now that Charlie's taken such a shine to your nose, uh, I mean, to you." I must blush fiercely because he looks ashamed. "Sorry, that just slipped out, you know because of the way you and Charlie rubbed noses and..." He trails off in embarrassment.

"Nice out, Rudy," Silverman says with a shake of his head.

The unintended insult doesn't bother me. My brain has already rewound to the beginning of my play time with Charlie and my heart beats blissfully as I watch it play out.

I shake Bell's hand. "See you soon."

Then I head back across the lab toward the exit.

Silverman speed walks to catch up.

Chapter 13

Nobody Move!

I'm barely aware of the ride back because I keep replaying in an endless loop the pure joy of being fully accepted by another living thing. I don't want to lose that feeling, no matter how many more remarks I have to endure about my nose or how some klutzy thing I did as a little kid made somebody laugh, so I savor every second of the memories I re-run through my mind's eye.

Silverman texted Ari when he left and said to meet behind St. Mary's. I also texted Ari that I was unharmed and had lots to tell him.

Ari's waiting when we pull up to the rear of St. Mary's, near the alley where all this started yesterday morning. Not only Ari, either, I notice as the replay in my brain winds down for the fourth time. Kash and Barn are with him. And... Mom? Oh, no, I'm in *big* trouble!

Silverman's driver eases the black sedan to a stop in front of the waiting group clustered around Ari's SUV, parked with its headlights on because it's getting dark.

Silverman glances over at me. "Quite a welcoming committee."

I'm barely able to swallow. Mom is gonna kill me!

"Let me do the talking," Silverman says, and I nod eagerly.

We exit the car and Mom swoops down on me like an eagle going after a rat, almost crushing me—again—with her strong arms. Ari is close behind, his hand on my shoulder, giving that familiar squeeze that comforts me.

"I'm okay, Mom," I splutter because I can barely breathe. She has my nose crushed against her body. No jokes, please.

She pulls back and glares at me, her eyes filled with equal parts fury and worry. "You are so grounded, mister!"

Silverman steps forward, hand extended. "I'm Oscar Silverman, Mrs. Fitzroy. I must commend you on raising such a fine boy."

His words seem to take the wind out of her bluster, most likely from the compliment. She shakes his hand.

"Thank you, Mr. Silverman. But Elmo knows better than to go off with strangers."

Silverman smiles, and it looks genuine. He pulls something from his front jacket pocket and hands one to Mom and one to Ari. They are business cards.

"As you can see, I run an agency within the Department

of Homeland Security. Mo was perfectly safe with me, and he has proven to be of tremendous help to us. I'm grateful to him and to you."

His calm, pleasant tone seems to soothe Mom even more and she glances down at the card in her hand. "You work for N.O.S.E?"

I groan. They never told me the name of the agency. I lean in toward Ari and he tilts the card in my direction. Under 'Department of Homeland Security', it says, 'National Office of Scientific Enquiry' and after that 'N.O.S.E.'

"An unfortunate acronym," Silverman says apologetically, glancing at me.

I'm probably turning red again as I pull my hair down over my face.

"I didn't mention it to Mo since he's rather sensitive on the subject. But you must admit, there's a certain irony in the name, given our association with your boy."

Kash and Barn move to flank me, and I push the awkwardness aside.

"Mom, Ari, I have to tell you about Charlie."

Mom holds up a hand in that 'talk to the hand' gesture she uses when I'm about to launch into a replay of events, but I'm too excited to heed her warning.

"Mom, this is *really* important."

"Mo, I'm talking with this man." Her tone is icy because I'm embarrassing her.

I'm shifting from side to side like I have to pee, but I don't.

I just need to verbally unwind what I rewound in my mind, and I can't wait too long when that need comes over me. My brain goes into overload and then I feel like it might short out.

"Ari, I *need* to tell you!"

He squeezes my shoulder again. "Okay, Mo, I've got you. Say goodbye to Mr. Silverman before we start."

I know it's his way of redirecting me and it works this time because I need to know when I can go back. I turn to Silverman. "Thank you *so* much for today. You don't know what it means to me."

Silverman wears the same stoic expression, but his eyes flicker with understanding. "I think I have an idea, Muppit Boy."

Mom gasps, but I break into a huge grin.

"Can I come back tomorrow? Please?"

Silverman glances at Mom while I bounce up and down on my heels.

"Please, Mom? I *have* to see Charlie again."

Mom frowns. "Who's Charlie? A boy you met?"

I shake my head. "No, Mom. Charlie's the condor that saved me yesterday."

"A bird?"

Her facial expression is so funny that Kash and Barn laugh.

"Charlie is a rather special bird, ma'am," Silverman puts in, drawing Mom's attention to him. "And he's formed quite an attachment to your son. You'd be helping us, and if

I may say so, you'd be helping Mo, if you allow him to spend more time with Charlie. Because condors are anomalous to this area, it would be best if he visited at our headquarters."

Mom is about to say no. I see it in the set of her mouth and the squint of her eyes.

I leap forward and grab her hand. "Mom, please, you have to let me!"

She looks mystified. "What's so special about a bird?"

I blush, hoping it's too dark for anyone to see. "He loves me, Mom, just like I am. He loves my nose."

She pulls back. "Your nose is beautiful, Mo," Mom says because she's a mother and kids are always beautiful to mothers.

"No, it's not. And I'm not cute or handsome like you always say. I'm goofy-looking, and you have thousands of comments on your YouTube channel to prove it." She gasps again, but I keep going. "Charlie likes my nose, Mom, maybe cause his is big, too, I don't know, but he likes me and doesn't expect me to be anything *but* me. I can't even tell you how that feels. Please, Mom, I *need* to go back!"

Mom has this look on her face that I've never seen before. It's like she's seeing a great truth she's been missing all her life.

Ari steps to her side. He's looking at me, meeting my gaze straight on like he always does, but he talks to Mom.

"I think he should go, Abigail. If it makes you feel better,

I'll go with him." He faces Silverman. "Will that work for you?"

I turn to Silverman. "Please?"

He studies Ari. "Like Mo, you will not know the location of our headquarters. My agency is involved in some of the most sensitive scientific research and development in this country."

Ari studies him right back. "That's fine. Long as I'm with my boy."

Now everyone looks at Mom. I still hold her hand in mine. I squeeze it gently, but firmly.

"I *need* this, Mom, more than I've ever needed anything."

Her face seems to clear, like she's been somewhere else, almost like me when I'm in rewind mode.

"I'm sorry, Mo, for everything. Of course, you can visit Charlie whenever Mr. Silverman says it's all right."

I release her hand and throw both arms around her in an intense hug. She wraps hers around me, but she's trembling, like she's nervous or scared.

"Well, I must be going," says Silverman from behind me.

I release Mom and turn. "I'll see you tomorrow. Can you put my number in your cell?

Silverman slips out his phone and I rattle off my number.

Silverman returns the phone to his pants pocket. "I'll text you, Mo."

He retreats into the darkened rear seat of his sedan and

closes the door. The car pulls away, rounding the corner out of sight.

We stand a moment in silence, as though no one knows what to say. But my brain hasn't forgotten where it left off. I spin around to Ari.

"Now can I tell you about Charlie?"

He smiles. "Of course. I think we'd all like to hear your story."

I start to talk, but Ari holds up a hand. "In the car, though."

Ari leads Mom toward his SUV while Barn claps me on the back. "You get to have all the fun."

I feel a hand on my other shoulder and let Barn move on ahead as I turn to find Kash looking at me strangely. I can't really describe it, but it's like she's looking at someone else and I happen to be blocking her view.

"I think your nose is perfect just the way it is."

Acting almost unnerved, Kash hurries to the car, leaving me to wonder what that was all about.

I scurry forward, anxious to tell everyone about Charlie, when suddenly, bright headlights spring to life all around us and I'm momentarily blinded.

A voice calls out of the darkness, "Nobody move!"

Chapter 14

I Guess You Want Your Family to Die

I squint against the light, barely able to make out Ari reaching underneath his jacket—for his gun, I'm sure. I hear a whizzing sound and then something small strikes Ari in the neck. He grunts and swats a hand at the area under his chin.

"Don't hit the Muppit kid!" the same voice shouts.

Ari begins to sag, but he manages to glance my way. "Mo...run!"

I'm paralyzed, but I don't want to leave my family. Kash runs forward and leaps into a flying kick. There's a loud grunt as her feet connect with the silhouette of a big man. The man stumbles back and Kash lands on her feet, fists raised to fight. But then another whizzing sound passes me, and I see Kash swat at her neck. She staggers a moment before toppling.

More whizzing noises fly past and Mom and Barn crumple to the pavement. This all happens in seconds. I focus on Ari on the ground, slumped against the bumper of his SUV. The headlight beam glares against one side of his face and makes him look hellish.

"I can't leave you guys!" I blurt as heavy footfalls pelt in my direction.

"Run!" spits Ari with his final breath before going limp.

The running footsteps close in on me from all sides. I spin around and confront a big, mean-looking guy who looks like a professional boxer. He's bald, his forearms look like tree branches, his ears stick out more than my nose, and his mouth is curled into a snarl.

"Come quietly, little boy. The boss doesn't want you hurt." His voice sounds like ice grinding in a blender.

I glance around me, my brain recording every detail. I'm surrounded by three men, including Mr. Ice Grinder in front of me. I can't fight my way out like Kash tried to, so I need to use my brain. I have nothing to throw, so the only thing I can do is run. I scan the distance between each man—it looks like they are a good six feet apart. But as they move steadily closer, the circle tightens. Within moments, it will be impossible for me to scurry through.

Mr. Ice Grinder takes several steps toward me, his legs spread apart like he's anchoring himself to the ground. The others close in. I do the only thing possible—I break into a run straight at Mr. Ice Grinder. He clearly wasn't expecting that move because his mouth shifts from a smirking snarl to a "O" of surprise. His arms reach out to grab me and that's when I duck. His hands swing above me so close I can feel the air moving, but I already have my head down and ram it into his groin. He bellows like wounded rhino and doubles over, allowing me to drop and skitter between his long legs. Sometimes being short is a good thing.

I run for the corner.

"He's getting away!"

I don't turn to look, but thudding footsteps on pavement tell me all I need to know. I barrel around the corner of St. Mary's and dash off the sidewalk into the parking lot. I have no idea where I'm going, but I scan every direction for an escape route or a place to hide as I approach the entrance to the school. The yellow caution tape is still strung across it. An overhang juts from the second floor, extending out over the front walkway.

As I race past the caution tape, I spot a ladder resting up against the side of the overhang. Like a monkey, I'm up that ladder and onto the overhang faster than I ever thought possible. I press back against the second-floor windows just as the men pelt around the corner and into the parking lot. They pass beneath the streetlight and, I notice, with some satisfaction, that Mr. Ice Grinder is limping.

Desperate for an escape route, I turn to find an open window. I clamber up over the sill into Sister Ella's science room. It looks like a bomb went off in there. Sammy left no test tube unturned. The splintered desks have been piled into one corner for disposal. I look across the darkened room to see that the hallway door is gone. I guess Sammy smashed it up and the workers removed it for safety. Whatever the reason, I bolt across the room, duck under the caution tape, and dart into the hall.

It looks even creepier at night than it does during the day. I glance both ways because there are stairs leading to the first floor at either end. The classroom doors are all closed—and probably locked—so my best bet is to hurry down the stairs and try to sneak out the back. Most likely, I'll have to climb out a window because those can be opened from the inside.

I scurry past doors and walls decorated with colorful artwork and photos of previous graduating classes. At the top of the stairs, in the corner, is a statue of the Virgin Mary looming in the darkness, reaching for me with ceramic hands draped by a blue ceramic veil. I scoot past her and race down the stairs. My footfalls echo in the empty building, and I'll be real easy to locate if those guys find a way in.

This place is cold and dangerous-looking and I stop at the bottom stair to glance from side to side. I realize my breaths are raspy and my heart is pounding. But my brain is on high-alert mode and records every detail of my surroundings. I dart across the hall to the back door and press gently against the restraining bar. It's key-locked, as I suspected. I retreat to the hall and look both ways. This floor has offices and classrooms, and my brain struggles to recall any standalone windows. I think back to the last time I walked down this hallway and call up those memories. I know I need to hurry, but the replay is short and I "see" the entire length of the hall without moving an inch.

There's a large window looking out onto the rear parking lot at the far end, right beside the other staircase. I launch myself into a sprint and race past the principal's office and some classrooms before passing the second set of shadowy stairs.

The window appears just ahead. Moonlight streams through and I hug the wall as I scoot toward it. If those guys are outside, I don't want them to see me. I halt just before reaching the window and peer through the glass. A streetlight casts the parking lot in a misty glow that, combined with the moonlight, looks especially scary, but I don't see anyone out there.

I extend one trembling hand and fiddle with the window latch. It has a short handle that slides to one side, raising the piece of metal that sticks into the wood of the sill to keep the window secured. These windows are old and slide upward in the frames.

The latch is stuck!

I'm forced to step away from the wall, putting myself in plain sight of anyone entering the parking lot. I need both hands to move the latch slowly to the right and I'm actually sweating by the time it clicks over, freeing the window. I plant a note in my brain for later rewind – work out more with Ari. I must be the weakest twelve-year-old on earth!

The window is also stuck—or I'm too weak—and I need to press both palms against the wooden base and push upward with my entire body, using my legs for leverage, to force the stupid thing to rise!

Clambering awkwardly up onto the sill, I feel my sneakers scrabbling for purchase on the smooth wall underneath and I dangle a moment, half in and half out of the window. I pull and push with my arms, but I misjudge how much pressure is required and topple right out the window into a flower bed, crushing Sister Anna's daisies and petunias.

I roll over and stumble to my feet. My hoodie is covered with dirt and bright yellow flower petals, but that's not what catches my eye. The three men turn the corner of the building and spot me.

"There he is!" It's Mr. Ice Grinder.

I leap from the flower bed and sprint across the parking lot toward the street. If I can get to one of the neighboring houses, maybe someone will help me. Mr. Ice Grinder breaks off from the group and angles his run toward me. One of the other guys changes his trajectory to circle around my other side. They're trying to trap me between them!

I stop, panting with fear. A distraction. That's what I need. And then it comes to me. I look up past the men toward the night sky behind them, forcing myself to stay focused.

Then I open my eyes wide and burst into a huge grin. "Charlie!"

Without titling my head down, I lower my gaze slightly and see the two men in front of me with their heads turned, obviously searching the sky behind them for whatever it is I'm seeing. That's when I lunge forward. They start to turn back, but I'm already there and dart between them. Hands flail out to grab me, but I'm too short—a good thing for the second time tonight—and I clear the men before they can recover from their surprise.

"I guess you want your family to die," says a voice behind me, and I skid to a halt.

Heart hammering, my breathing raspy, I turn around. The men haven't moved. Mr. Ice Grinder wears a nasty leer.

"What do you mean?"

"The boss wants *you*," Mr. Ice Grinder growls. "The others are just leverage. If we fail to deliver you, he won't need them anymore."

He slides a brutal-looking knife from a sheath on his belt and holds it out so the streetlight glints off its serrated blade. "That means they're mine to dispose of."

"No! You can't hurt my family!"

The man shrugs and waves the knife around. "That depends on you, Muppit Boy."

I know Ari said to run, but there's no way I'll leave my family to die if there's anything I can do to stop it. Besides, once I get to their headquarters, maybe I can think of an escape plan.

"Okay. You win."

I lumber forward on feet that feel as though they're made of lead. I'm scared and I'm not afraid to admit it. Yeah, the Boy Code says boys are never supposed to admit they're scared or weak, but I'm both right now, especially as I draw nearer to that massive knife that looks like it could turn me into pepperoni slices with just a few swings.

I stop beneath the streetlight a few feet from Mr. Ice Grinder and look up at him, fighting to keep my face neutral. Boy Code or not, there's no good reason to show the bad guys I'm scared.

Mr. Ice Grinder eyes me under the light and then whistles in amazement. "Man, you are one ugly kid."

I stiffen but force myself not to react.

"Check this kid out under the light, guys," he says to the others.

They saunter over and peer down at me like I'm a zoo exhibit.

"Is that the ugliest kid you ever saw or what?"

One of the men chortles. "I could sure use that nose in my backyard. Be a perfect leaf blower."

Mr. Ice Grinder laughs.

My fear spirals into anger. "You guys won't win any beauty contests, either," I snarl, fighting to keep my brain from sliding off the table. I glower at Mr. Ice Grinder. "Good thing you got those Dumbo ears. If the car steering goes out, we can drive the rest of the way using them."

The other two laugh at my insult, but one feral look from Mr. Ice Grinder shuts them down. He steps so close to me we practically touch and then bends down to lock eyes with me. I'm too mad to cower. He holds the knife out, but I don't even flinch. He brings it to my throat. I glare at him like a rabid dog and don't back away.

"You better hope the boss decides to keep you around, Muppit Boy," Mr. Ice Grinder says in a low, rumbling voice. "Because I'd like nothing better than to make your face even uglier than it is now."

I can't help myself. When this kind of mood strikes, my sarcasm meter swings into overdrive. "If you want a template for ugliness when you rearrange my face, look in a mirror."

He flinches and the blade nicks my throat. I don't react, even when a trickle of blood rolls down my neck.

He pulls the knife back. "Your tongue will go first." He looks like he's mad enough to gut me there and then but manages to regain control and sheath the knife. "Take him."

The other two men step forward to grab one arm each and practically carry me to a four-door sedan with the logos removed and no license plates. I'm tossed into the backseat like I'm one of those Muppit Boy dolls, and the doors are slammed. There's a glass divider separating the front from the rear and no handles on the insides of the doors.

The two men take up positions in the front seat and one

of them twists his head around to face me. "Sleep well, kid. Maybe you'll dream you're not so ugly." He laughs and reaches for a button on the dashboard.

There's a hissing sound, but I don't see anything. A smell assails my nostrils, not unpleasant, but definitely not something I've smelled before. Drowsiness overwhelms me. Just before everything goes dark, I realize that the hissing is some kind of knockout gas. And then I'm gone.

Chapter 15

What Did You Do to Me?

I wake up slowly. My brain feels like it's filled with lead. In fact, my whole body seems heavy and unfamiliar. I open my eyes and blink a few times. Fluorescent lights glow above me and I glance from side to side. I'm in some sort of lab, but my brain is still too fuzzed up from whatever they knocked me out with to bring the details into clear focus.

I try to sit up, but I can't. Dread clutches my heart and I look down at my body. I'm strapped to a table. No, more like a hospital gurney of some kind. I try to move my hands, but both wrists, and both ankles, are secured to the table with strong, leather restraints.

Okay, this is when I freak out. I've never felt this kind of panic and I kick and yank at the restraints, even though my brain tells me it's a wasted effort.

Except it isn't.

Snap!

My right hand is free. I stare in shock at the restraint that's now torn from the table like it was made of paper. I don't know how I did it, but my heart thrums with excitement and I yank the other wrist strap loose. It rips open at the buckle.

What the...?

I'm too keyed up to think clearly. Two strong kicks of my legs and I free both of my ankles, leaving the leather straps torn and useless.

I leap off the gurney and stumble. Reaching out, I grab the nearest countertop to steady myself, fighting to clear my head. I feel weird. I know that's not very descriptive for a detective, but it fits. My entire body seems...different, like it isn't mine anymore. I steady myself and take inventory. I'm still wearing the same tee shirt and shorts, minus my hoodie. That's good, right? I realize I can see clearly, but I don't feel...I reach up for my glasses. They're gone. Then I spot them neatly folded up atop the counter, not three feet from my hands. That's crazy! I've worn glasses my whole life! How can I see without them?

I study my arms and hands. They look the same. I roll up the sleeve on my right arm and examine the biceps. Still skinny as a broom handle. Not sure why, I flex and feel the muscle. I almost gasp in surprise. It feels hard, not soft like before, but it doesn't look any different.

My brain is still fogged and there's a slight throbbing, like the beginnings of a headache.

What did they do to me?

I scan the lab. There are two monitors on the wall before me and I gasp when I see what's displayed on them. Both monitors show the inside of what look like jail cells, complete with bars. On one monitor I see Barn and Kash and the other shows Mom and Ari. Mom is sitting on a bench crying while Ari paces. Barn and Kash stand at the bars looking out. I see them talking, but there's no sound. I search around the controls and spot a switch that says, 'Audio'. I twist it and suddenly Barn's voice fills the lab.

"...always stood up for me, since the first grade, even though he got punked for it. When we were little, the Muppit Boy thing made him cool with other kids. But standing up for me, the fat, clumsy kid, that's what ruined his rep. I owe him everything, Kash."

Kash places a hand on his shoulder. "We're gonna save him, and us. I've got an idea. Remember what you did in the shoe store?"

Barn looks at her, clearly embarrassed. "You mean I tripped over everything?"

She grins. "Exactly. I have a feeling they'll move us from these cells, and when they do..." She leans down and whispers in his ear. I strain but can't pick up anything she says. But when she pulls back, Barn grins. After that, they fall silent and stare out through the bars at something I can't see from this angle.

I stand there stunned, replaying Barn's words in my mind. He made me sound like some kind of hero just for being his friend. Sure, he was the most unpopular kid at St. Mary's from the get-go and I guess I felt sorry for him. But being his friend has been the best thing ever. Sure, we're both losers, but we're losers who have each other's back and that means the world.

I twist the volume knob for the other monitor. Now Ari's voice fills the lab.

"...let anything happen to him, Abigail. You know I'd die for that boy."

He's sitting beside Mom on the bench with one arm around her shoulders. I've never seen either of them look so fragile. I always thought of them as Titans who would protect me from everything. But maybe they can't....

"I can't lose him, Aristotle," Mom says, her voice hitching with emotion. "He's my everything."

My heart lurches in my chest. I hate seeing my mother cry, so I turn off the audio. Anger consumes me that all of this is happening. I'm gripping the edge of the fiberglass counter when a sudden *snap* startles me. I look down in horror to see chucks of the countertop in each hand.

Huh?

Shaking with fear, I drop the pieces and spin around. What

is this place? Computer screens abound, but there are also rolling tables with surgical instruments on them. That sends a chill up and down my back. Did I get operated on? I yank up my shirt to check my chest and abs—well, my torso, anyway. I have no pecs and no visible abs. I see no incisions, so that's good.

I have a sudden impulse to punch myself in the midsection. I expect my fist to sink in or, if I punch hard enough, to knock the wind out of me. But my fist strikes solid flesh, and I mean *solid.* I increase the pressure, pounding against my invisible abs. I barely feel any pain, and the only effect is a reddening of the skin where my fist struck.

What is going on here?

I lower my shirt, fighting down a wave of panic. Something has changed inside of me. I feel it. My brain is aware, but my mind hasn't caught up yet.

They did something to me!

Feeling steady on my feet now, I cross to the door and grip the knob. It's locked. Maybe it's the panic coursing through me or maybe something else, but I squeeze the knob and twist. It snaps off in my hand and the door drifts open.

I stare at the broken knob in stunned silence. Not only did it break off, but I notice indentations in the metal where my fingers applied pressure.

A coldness sweeps over me, and my brain starts shifting into overload mode. I fight against it. I must stay in control, despite fear attacking me from all sides and making me weak in the knees.

I take deep breaths. In and out. In and out. A semblance of calm fills my being, enough to toss the knob to the floor and push my way through the door.

I'm inside a secondary lab with only computers and workstations and there's another door across the way. Unfortunately, that door is blocked by three of the goons who kidnapped me, including Mr. Ice Grinder.

I should be scared, but I'm not. Maybe it's the whole "you just broke a doorknob off with one hand" thing, but rather than retreat, I step closer.

"Where's my family?"

"The boss said we could have our way with you and that's what we're gonna do," Mr. Ice Grinder snarls as he holds up that hunting knife.

The guy to his right lunges for me, fist raised for what looks like a killing blow. My brain clicks over, almost like switching to a new chapter on a DVD, and I "see" the punch striking my left cheek before it's even thrown. By the time the goon actually swings his fist, I've ducked and his hand sails over my head. I anchor my feet and slam outwards with my fist—making sure to keep my wrist straight like Ari taught me—and connect with his midsection. I expect to feel like I've hit a wall—I know what walls feel like from past temper tantrums—but this man's midsection caves in like a giant marshmallow. He utters a startled grunt and stumbles back into the other two. They try to support him, but the man struggles to breathe and collapses at their feet, gasping and clutching his midsection, face twisted in pain.

I don't even have time to react before my brain "shows" Mr. Ice Grinder rushing forward and plunging the sharp, gleaming knife at me. Again, I "see" the blade sinking into my chest and leap backward before it can. The blade swings wildly past in a *whoosh* of air and then I'm kicking out with one foot, connecting with the man's groin and sending him to the floor in a howl of agony. The knife goes flying and he clutches his privates, rolling around like he'll never get up again.

I face off against the third guy. He's shorter than the other two, with forearms the size of ham hocks and brass knuckles wrapped around both sets of fingers. Once again, I "see" what's going to happen before it does. He jumps toward me, swinging up with his right fist and connecting with my jaw, which I know will shatter if those knuckles hit me. But I've already stepped to one side and stuck out my right leg. His fist swings wide at the same moment his feet catch on my leg. He topples forward, landing in a heap across Mr. Ice Grinder. With an animal growl, the short guy starts to rise, swinging out one arm toward me. Wrapping my fists together, I hammer them down on his arm as hard as I can. There's an audible *crack* and the man screams in torment.

I pull my fists back, staring at them in horror.

The man collapses and moans in pain, his wild eyes regarding me venomously. "Stupid punk, you broke my arm!"

"I didn't mean to!" I blurt, my body taut with fear.

What's happened to me?

Before I can do anything else, I hear clapping behind me. I whirl around and face a guy who looks like a cross between Darth Vader and Dr. Doom from *The Fantastic Four*—assuming those guys secretly dreamed of being a pharmacist. He's short, probably not much over five eight, wearing black dress shoes with a black shirt and pants and an open white pharmacist smock like the kind I see all the time on the CVS workers who fill my mom's prescriptions. Over that is draped a massive white cloak, and covering his face is a large gold mask with slits for eyeholes, small openings for breathing, and a slash for a mouth. The cloak hood covers the back of his head and top of the mask, so no hair is visible.

"Very impressive performance, Muppit Boy," he says, the voice sounding tinny, like it's coming from inside a washing machine. "Better than I expected." He regards the three men rolling on the floor in various stages of incapacitation. "Looks I'll need to recruit replacements."

Despite those men trying to kill me—twice—I feel terrible for what I did.

"I didn't mean to hurt them." I focus on the man before me and fight to maintain control. "You're Dr. Drug."

"At your service," he replies with a bow. "I'm honored to finally meet the famous Muppit Boy in person. I confess I'm not much for YouTube, but you have always been my favorite. The best episode, hands down, was when you tried to climb onto your mother's dressing table and knocked all her hair accessories on top of you." He chortles. "Remember? You ended up with a hair clip attached to your nose. I almost died from laughter."

I squirm with anger but shove it to the back of my brain. I can't let him get to me. "At least I don't walk around pretending to be Darth Vader."

"The noted Muppit Boy sarcasm. How I've missed that since you left the show. It's sad, really. Your mother lost over a million followers when you quit."

My breath hitches in my throat. Mom never told me that. How does he know? But it doesn't matter. What matters now is *finding* Mom.

"Where's my family?"

"You saw the monitors, so you know they're alive," he replies, ignoring my question. "For how long depends on you."

"What do you mean?"

He steps away from the open door and extends one arm. "Allow me to show you around. We can talk on the way."

I study him for any sign of weapons but can't tell if any are lurking beneath the cloak.

"In answer to your thought, I am not armed," he wheezes through the mask. "I have no need. Attacking me will only hasten the deaths of your beloved family and friends."

I sag slightly. "Okay."

I step forward, circling around the injured men, and walk past Dr. Drug through the open door.

Between his weird costume and the corridor I step into, I get the definite feeling he's obsessed with *Star Wars*. The ceilings are low, the walls black and metallic-looking, and people wearing gray jumpsuits walk past in both directions. Dr. Drug steps up beside me and his cape rustles against my back.

"Ask your questions, Muppit Boy. Let's see how good a detective you've become."

"Why'd you take my family if it was me you wanted?"

"We'll get there eventually."

The know-it-all tone of voice annoys me.

"How did you know I want to be a detective?"

People pass us and bow their heads at Dr. Drug like he's some kind of emperor or something.

"I know everything about you," he replies, his voice echoing in the hallway.

"You and everyone else," I mutter, fighting my annoyance and focusing on the various rooms we pass. Most have large viewing windows and seem to be labs, maybe for doctors to do research, though none look set up for surgeries like the one I woke up in.

"How long have I been here?"

"Thirty-six hours, give or take. You recovered from the procedure more quickly than I anticipated."

A chill envelops me. "What did you do to me?"

"I've made you better, Muppit Boy. Couldn't you tell that

much after escaping my surgical chamber and defeating three seasoned assassins?"

"What did you do to me?" I repeat, my voice tight and low.

"Use that bear trap of a brain you have and figure it out for yourself. You won't be much of a detective if you can't see past the nose on your face." He laughs. "Oh, yes, you can never see *that* far, can you?"

He laughs, but I don't rise to the bait. Instead, I think about everything I've learned over the past few days. I think about what I just did to those men who kidnapped me. I think about Sammy and Charlie, the old people with the chainsaws, and all I learned from Bell and Silverman.

And then I know.

"You made me nanonic like those old people, didn't you?"

I can scarcely breathe at the thought. I sense, rather than see, a smile behind the shiny gold mask.

"Indeed, except you, Muppit Boy, are a vastly superior upgrade. You were always the perfect child for my needs. Smart, clever, and with a unique brain under all that hair. And it didn't hurt that I loved your show." He chuckles. "I've placed within you the most recent nanonic updates, the genius of my research, the very research stolen from me by Silverman and Bell."

"Huh?"

"Come, come, Muppit Boy," he says in that smug tone. "You met Bell. Clearly, he's not capable of such a creation as

Charlie without help. It was my discovery that led to nanonics, but I was just a lowly lab tech with a brilliant mind. When he stole my discovery, and claimed it for himself, what could I do?"

My feet feel heavy as I tromp along the corridor next to him. If he's telling the truth, does that mean I can't trust Bell and Silverman either?

"I was terminated shortly thereafter, but I took my knowledge with me and began anew. I spent several years behind the scenes at one of the largest pharmaceutical companies in the world, siphoning off millions of R & D dollars into an offshore account."

"R & D?"

"Research and development," he replies as we circle around and continue walking.

I begin to realize that this corridor isn't straight – it's circular.

"I used that money to invest in other pharmaceuticals until I set up my own clandestine labs around the world. No one knows my true identity. Just as you are forever Muppit Boy, I am forever Dr. Drug."

I glare at him. "Muppit Boy is a character. I'm not."

He sniggers and it sounds like marbles rolling around inside a tin can. "Thanks to the Internet, once you have an identity with the general public, that's who you'll always be. And the people want *you* to be Muppit Boy."

I should argue with him, but I know there's no point. First

of all, it won't change his mind. And second, he's right. I *will* be Muppit Boy for the rest of my life. I skirt that unpleasant thought and focus on the nanonics. I tremble at the understanding that I've been fundamentally changed.

"What exactly did you put inside me?"

He rubs his hands together with glee. It's like I'm watching the Grinch.

"You, Muppit Boy, are my greatest creation. Being on the verge of adolescence, your bones are porous, your muscles supple and ready for the influx of testosterone to make them thicker. My nanites have infused your bones and muscles, filling in every possible space, giving you strength enough to take down grown men. And your body can sustain a substantial amount of abuse before you even bruise. Your skin is thicker and stronger. But the best part is your brain. My nanites have enhanced your brain tenfold. You might have noticed that during the fight."

I rewind my brain to when the fight began and see myself reacting to the punches before they occurred. "That's why you let them attack me, because you knew I'd win."

"Of course."

I feel queasy and light-headed. "It's twisted and wrong."

"Haven't you been a joke long enough? I've reinvented you. I've made you the most powerful boy on the planet and a force to be reckoned with. Together, you and I will rule the world."

"I'll never help you."

He peers at me from behind the mask. "If you refuse, your family will die. At your hands, by the way."

"Never!" My brain spins round and round with all this new information. Kill my family? I could never do that.

"Let's pay them a visit, shall we?"

I nod because I'm too afraid to speak. I'm too afraid, period. He made me something that's not quite human anymore. I want to cry. My entire life has been a joke and now this?

I fight against the sadness, struggling to keep my brain in recording mode as we walk in case the footage might be useful later. My eyes sweep from side to side, taking in every detail of the labs and the workers who stroll past.

"Are there other nanonic people besides me?"

"Just Billy and Polly," he responds. "I experimented on them first because, well, let's face it, they're old. If they died during the procedure, it's not like they weren't at death's door anyway."

I shudder again. I never thought much about murderers except how to catch them. But the way this man talks about people like they're used sandwich bags that can just be thrown away chills my blood. Another question spins around my head.

"Where are we, anyway? This looks like the inside the Death Star."

Drug chortles, and hollowness of it unnerves me.

"We are beneath the hills on the west coast of Santa

Catalina Island. During World War II, a secret labyrinth of bunkers was built here to house thousands of troops should Japan attempt a coastal invasion. I discovered the location while working for Silverman. He didn't even know it existed and it's been long abandoned by the government. Using my security clearance, I erased all records of its existence and over a number of years reconfigured the bunkers into this."

Now that he's told me what used to be here, I can see the basic shape of what was probably concrete, but he covered it all over with a façade of plastic lining.

"But why the Death Star?"

He shrugs. "I'm a geek, what can I say?"

"Seriously? A super-villain geek?" I can't help the sarcasm.

He laughs. "That's my Muppit Boy."

"I'm not *your* Muppit Boy!"

"Oh, but you are," he replies as we approach several cells with bars across the front. "You just don't know it yet."

His words are lost on me as we stop, and I see who's inside the closest cell.

"Mom!"

Chapter 16

You Turned Me Into A Drone?

My mother is sitting hunched over on a bench that's attached to the back wall, I guess for the occupant to use as a bed. Ari paces back and forth. In the adjoining cell, Barn and Kash sit on their bench looking morose.

"Mo!"

Mom leaps to her feet and darts for the bars, reaching through for me. Ari grins with obvious relief as I take Mom's hand and grip it gently. After what I did to those men, I need to be careful how hard I do anything. I let go before Mom can feel my fingers trembling.

"Are you all right, honey?" Mom's been crying. Her eyes are red and puffy, just like I saw on the monitor.

Should I tell her the truth, that I'm anything *but* all right? No, that would make her feel worse.

"I'm good, Mom. Dr. Doom back here hasn't hurt me." I toss a thumb back at Drug.

"If you touch a hair on my boy's head, you'll answer to me." Ari rears up like a grizzly bear ready to attack. If the bars weren't there, I swear he'd pounce.

Drug shakes his masked head in amusement. "I have no intention of harming my greatest creation, Detective. And I must point out that he's no longer *your* boy. He's mine."

Mom throws a hand to her mouth.

Kash grips the bars of her cell. "He is *so* not yours!"

Ari looks from Drug to me with his searching detective gaze. "What's he talking about, Mo?"

I don't know how to answer, partly because I don't *know* the full answer. Instead, I turn to Drug. "You said you wouldn't hurt my family, so prove it and let them go."

"You need a demonstration first, Muppit Boy."

Drug raises one hand and snaps his fingers at two uniformed men walking past. They veer over to stand before the doctor, stiff and at attention. They are both young, I note, not more than thirty, tall and thick and powerful-looking. Both sport wide chests and meaty arms. I shudder at the thought of them roughing up my family, or worse.

Dr. Drug points to the man with the larger hands. Seriously, each hand looks bigger than my head!

"You, extend your right hand."

The man does so immediately.

Drug addresses the second man. "You, grip him from behind so he doesn't fall."

Uncertainty flits across the faces of both men as they assume the indicated positions.

Drug slides a smartphone from somewhere beneath his voluminous cloak and eyes me with a tilt of his head. "Shake his hand, Muppit Boy."

Mystified, I step forward and extend my right hand. I feel the gazes of my family fixed on the scene with puzzled expectation. I place my small hand within the massive one of the man and watch it disappear. My fingers barely reach around his palm. I squeeze like I normally do while shaking hands.

From the corner of my eye, I spot Drug tapping his phone screen. "Now, Muppit Boy, you will crush his hand."

My mother gasps, and the man whose hand I grip flinches back in surprise.

"Do not let go!" Drug snaps at the man, and his grip once more closes over mine.

Without letting go of the hand, I turn my head to face Drug. "I wouldn't do that even if I could."

"You can and you will."

"No way."

I start to release my grip when Drug taps his phone again. I stiffen against my will. I have no control over my body. I lean toward the man, even though I don't want to. His eyes widen with fear. I squeeze his hand. I try not to, but I can't control my actions. The man squeezes back.

I want to let go and step back, but I only squeeze harder. And harder. Sweat breaks out on my forehead and drips down my nose, tickling me. My brain is on fire as I fight desperately for control of my body. The man grimaces and increases his pressure, but I squeeze with greater intensity, first matching his strength and then surpassing it. I can't stop! His fingers release their tension as he runs out of strength. But I keep going, harder and harder, gripping until my hand looks white and every little vein stands out.

And then I hear it, the sound that will haunt me forever.

Breaking bones.

The man cries out in agony, but I still can't let go.

"Stop it!" I rasp, barely able to speak.

The veins on my forearm are bulging. I never saw those before.

Then, just like that, I'm free. On its own, my hand opens, and the man drops to his knees, moaning with pain and clutching his hand to his chest.

"What did you do to Mo?" Ari sounds horrified.

I turn to Ari, my face twisted with revulsion, my heart racing. I need him to tell me I didn't just break a man's hand. I need him to tell me everything is going to be all right. But I know everything isn't going to be all right, and Ari's terrified look confirms that realization.

I look back at the whimpering man. "I'm sorry, I'm so sorry." Tears burn my eyes. "I didn't want to do that! I don't even know *how* I did that!"

The injured man glowers with a mix of pain and anger, but he looks at Dr. Drug, not me.

"Take him to the medical wing," Drug orders.

The other guy hesitates, like he's considering an attack on his boss, but then helps the wounded man to his feet.

Still cradling the injured hand against his body, the man glances at me with wide, teary eyes, but doesn't look angry or hateful. He looks like he's afraid for me. Then he's gone, led off down the corridor.

I whirl around, furious, and step right up to that creepy gold mask. "Why did you make me do that? How did you do that?"

I feel like I'm going to explode, and this time Ari can't place a hand on my shoulder to help me breathe.

Drug holds up his phone.

"I told you I could make you kill your family," he says smoothly. "Now you know it's true."

"What have you done to my son?" Mom grips the bars like she wants to rip them out.

"I merely literalized what you created."

Ari moves to Mom's side. "What are you talking about?"

"The boy's mother created a character out of her son, a puppet, if you will," Drug goes on, talking about me as though I'm not standing right there. "For her own self-aggrandizement, in a venal pursuit of fame. She turned his normal, clumsy childhood moments into fodder for small minds to glom onto. Muppit Boy, with his big nose and penchant for falling over things, took a mediocre YouTube channel with a handful of followers and turned it into a worldwide sensation. He was the puppet and his mother the puppeteer. Am I right, Abigail?"

I watch Mom, my breathing on hold. I'm waiting for her to deny it, to yell and scream that it's all lies. But the look she directs my way reeks of guilt and remorse.

I turn on Drug. "You take that back! You can't talk to my mother that way!"

I vaguely realize that I'm losing it. Everything that's happened since waking up in that lab is suffocating me and overloading my brain at the same time. My ADHD is about to blow up like an atomic bomb.

"You can see the truth on her face," Drug says, without the slightest change in tone. "I just took her creation one step further. I turned Muppit Boy into Puppet Boy." He holds up the phone and my spinning brain fights for focus. "I can control the nanites in your brain with an app on my phone and thus, force you to do anything I want."

My head feels like it will explode. "You turned me into a drone?"

That tin can laugh fills the corridor. "An apt analogy, Muppit Boy."

"Mo, stay calm," Ari calls, his voice penetrating the confusion of thoughts gyrating around in my head. "Deep breaths."

"We'll find a way to undo what you did!" That's Kash, leaping to my defense.

"Alas, you won't, little girl," Drug replies. "Muppit Boy and I have a deal, don't we?"

I force air into my lungs. I need to stay in control or my family will get hurt.

"Mo, what's he talking about?" That's Ari.

I look up to see all of them staring at me with fear and expectation. My mother looks like she's on her way to the electric chair.

I expel a deep breath. "I'm going to stay with him. If I do, he'll let you go."

"No!" Ari grips the bars and presses his face against them.

Mom focuses on Drug, her eyes filling with water. "You can't have my son. I won't allow it."

"As you just saw, Abigail," Drug says, holding out his phone, "I can easily have Muppit Boy kill you all. Can you imagine how that would weigh on his conscience? No, this is best for everyone."

"Not for Mo, it isn't," Kash shoots back.

"Yeah," Barn pipes up, sounding more fearless than I've ever heard him. "He's our friend, not yours."

I step right up to the bars. "Please. I can't let you all die." I look into my mother's tear-filled eyes. "I don't care what he said, Mom. I love you." I glance shyly at Kash and Barn and then at Ari. "I love all of you."

Mom reaches a hand through the bars and takes mine in hers. Her long fingers caress my hand like she always did when I was little. "I love you, Mo, more than anything. You know that, right?"

Tears well in my eyes and dribble down my cheeks. I nod because I don't trust myself to speak.

Ari steps forward and reaches out for my other hand. I flash back to when I was seven and my tiny hand would vanish within his whenever we'd cross streets or parking lots.

"I will get you back, Mo." His voice is low and tight, like he's about to break and doesn't want the others to see. I guess the Boy Code even applies to men who don't want it to.

"So, we have a deal?" Drug steps up and pulls my hands away from Mom and Ari. He turns me around, so I'm forced to look into those slits that hide his eyes.

"We have a deal," I mutter and look down, feeling gutted.

"Excellent."

He sweeps me around to his side with one arm before facing my mom and the others.

"I'll arrange to have you all escorted to the surface. You'll be given my sleeping gas, of course, so you can't find this location again. It's been a pleasure."

Planting one hand around the back of my neck, he leads the way down the corridor, away from the people I love more than anything in the world. I try to look back, but only catch a glimpse of my mother crying into Ari's shoulder before Drug forces me to turn away.

Chapter 17

I Will Never Write That

"How will I know you let them go?" I ask as we head to an unfamiliar section of the Death Star bunkers.

Only a few people pass me and these wear lab coats and what look like gas masks dangling from around their necks. I focus on my surroundings to block out images of that man's broken hand. My stomach clenches at the thought of what I did, and what I've been turned into.

"I have cameras everywhere," he says after a moment. "You can watch from the launch bay."

"Launch bay?"

"My rocket," he says casually, like everyone has a rocket lying around. "It's high time I explained my plans, so you'll have a better idea how I work."

"I already know about the allergies you've spread around, like the peanut and gluten ones."

He sniggers, obviously very pleased with himself. I want to knock that mask right off his face, but I wouldn't get far if I tried. He can tap his phone screen in seconds.

"They were brilliant, if I do say so myself." He laughs. "Those, however, were mere warmups. What I plan on launching today into the atmosphere will make me the richest, most powerful man on earth."

His tone scares me. What could he be launching into the atmosphere, a microorganism to make people allergic to money? Come to think of it, that might not be so bad. Then another question pops into my head. "What was up with those stolen hearing aids?"

He shrugs. "Another method for shipping microorganisms around the world undetected, mainly to third world countries where poor people have to sift through used hearing aids to find some that are a close enough match. My people on site remove the infected aids and release the microorganisms on my command."

My brain fills with horror. Is there no limit to this man's cruelty and greed? I consider the broken hearing aids I saw in the old folks' dungeon.

"What were the old people looking for?"

He gives me a long stare that creeps me out. "A particular hearing aid that was never intended to ship. It was stolen by a now-ex-employee of mine who thought he might blackmail me."

I'm almost afraid to ask but do. "Uh, what happened to him?"

"Let's just say the only creatures he can blackmail now are at the bottom of the ocean."

I try to swallow, but my throat is so dry I can barely breathe. I don't say more about the missing hearing aid because I already know it hasn't been found.

Drug stops in front of a door and punches a series of numbers onto a keypad at eye level. He thinks I can't see, just like Silverman, but his cloak lifts high enough as he types that I can peek under it. My brain records the numbers and files them away. I must stay focused on stopping this man any way I can, so I push aside all thoughts of my family for now.

The door slides open and Drug steps back for me to enter.

"Don't trust me?"

"Trust is earned," he replies, his voice sounding especially tinny in this corridor. "If I turn my back, you're likely to attempt something annoying, at the very least."

I lean in, offering my snarkiest expression. "I'm in middle school. I'm *supposed* to be annoying."

Unfortunately, he loves my sarcasm too much and just laughs. I'll have to find some other way to get under his skin.

Drug follows me inside, but I notice the door doesn't close behind him.

I've seen videos of space shuttle launches back when America sent them into space and watched tons of old moon launches with those huge Saturn V rockets. The room into which I step looks a lot like the NASA Mission Control Center in Houston. There's a long console with about a million buttons, many glowing white or red, while others are dark, like they're waiting to be fired up. Monitors fill the wall above the console and on those monitors, I see a rocket. The rocket isn't outdoors because there's no sky behind it. It's lit by artificial light and seems to be encased in a tube. Several people in lab coats work at the launch console and ignore us completely.

Across from the console is a massive computer station with a monitor the size of a movie screen. Okay, not that big, but almost. And standing in front of the computer, each brandishing a chainsaw, are the old couple who tried to kill me. The lady grins and the man waves his chainsaw back and forth like a flag.

"Pity we can't cut you up, Muppit Boy," she says in her sandpapery voice, "to make up for that pen trick, but you can still give me that autograph you promised."

I rear back. "I will never write that."

The old man laughs, sounding like a horse with a sore throat. "Never say never, sonny."

Dr. Drug leads me over to them. "Muppit Boy, let me formally introduce you to Polly and Billy, my first experiments in nanonics. Polly and Billy, I present the world's first nanonic boy."

He claps me on the back like we're old friends. I feel an urge to break his hand but bite it back. One day he's going to be *really* sorry he made me nanonic!

Polly holds up her chainsaw. "You might be stronger, faster, and younger, but we have these. A chainsaw is the great equalizer."

"Maybe," I grudgingly admit, but in the back of my mind I'm considering how I can get my hands on one of those chainsaws. I could do serious damage to the computer and launch console with one of them.

"Are the tanks ready to be loaded?" Drug asks Polly.

"Yes, indeedy, Doctor," she rasps enthusiastically.

"Uh." They all turn to look at me. "What microorganisms are you planning to launch in that rocket?"

"Bravo, Muppit Boy, on your deductive skills. I've included a smorgasbord of ten allergy-causing microorganisms. All are airborne, naturally, and will disperse over much of the world based on wind currents at the time of launch. One of those microorganisms will make people allergic to chocolate."

My eyes bug out. "That's horrible! What about all the kids who won't be able to eat birthday cake?"

"But they will be able to," Drug goes on, clearly proud of himself. "After their parents buy the special antihistamine my company will manufacture."

"That's sick!"

I find myself shaking with rage. How many parents can't

afford these drugs and their kids won't ever get to eat chocolate cake?

"It's just good business, Muppit Boy. You'll come to understand that when you're older."

"If understanding stuff like that is what getting older means, I'll stay twelve."

He laughs. "You children have such a simplistic view of life."

"Maybe. But I bet our simplistic view of life would work better than yours."

"You'll lose that innocence one day."

I force myself to stay calm. I need to find a way to disrupt his plans, or I'll have lost my family for nothing. "What else are you sending up?"

"Are you aware that Starbucks had over thirty-six billion dollars in revenue last year?"

"Uh, no, I don't read the stock pages."

"Think of the millions of people addicted to Starbucks. What would happen if, suddenly, they developed an allergy to the very coffee they can't live without?"

I think of how my Mom and her friends love Starbucks, and shiver. Mom gets pretty cranky without her coffee.

"I expect *that* antihistamine will outsell the chocolate one," Drug goes on, his metallic voice filled with delight. "If parents can only afford one, they'll take the coffee for sure and let their kids go without chocolate. They might even be happy their kids can't eat chocolate, so I could be doing an enormous favor for parents everywhere."

"Yeah, they can name you Dr. Nice Guy, instead of Dr. Doom Vader."

He claps me on the back again. "Love that sense of humor."

Polly and Billy laugh, too, but mostly to kiss up to their boss, I think.

"I probably don't want to know, but what's the worst one you're sending up?"

"Let's see if the great boy detective can figure it out. What's something so ubiquitous that virtually everyone on the planet uses it at least some of the time?"

I'm a well-read kid, but I don't know "ubiquitous." I grudgingly ask the meaning.

"It means found everywhere, sonny," Billy says like it's the most common word in the world.

I ignore his sarcasm and consider the question. "Have I used this thing you're targeting?"

"Unquestionably," Drug replies, focusing on me with that creepy mask and the piercing eyes watching from behind it.

I look around the room, hoping for a clue. I note the computers everywhere and have the sudden urge to look for cables. I duck down and peer under the computer tables, but I don't see any cords except the power plug.

And then I know. "Wi-Fi?"

Drug claps, despite the phone in one hand. "You're good, kid. I thought you'd need more clues."

"You can make people allergic to Wi-Fi?"

"Quite easily," he replies like we're talking about the plot of some TV show, rather than the potential enslavement of the human race. "And since no one can fully live without Wi-Fi, everyone will need *that* antihistamine, ensuring my status as the most powerful man on the planet. And you, Muppit Boy, will be my right-hand man. Well, *boy*, for now."

I'm stunned. Even at my age when I know so little about the adult world, I clearly see the big picture here and I can't let that rocket go off. But what can I do to stop it? I point at the people working the launch sequence.

"Are they in control of the rocket?" Drug gazes at me a long moment and I again feel creeped out at not being able to fully see his eyes. "Hey, I'm a detective, okay? I ask questions." I hope my snarky attitude will work, and it does.

"No," Drug replies, sounding rather smug. "The rocket controls itself. It's completely automated from an onboard computer, which means once the launch sequence is engaged, no one can stop it. Not even me."

I try my best to look impressed. "Very cool." I stare across the room at a solid steel wall that includes a door. "Is the rocket behind there?"

"Yes."

"Can I see it before it goes up?"

There's another long pause while he studies me.

"I'm a nerd." I offer my best smile. "And I've never seen a real rocket before."

Drug holds up his phone. "Remember your family."

I nod.

We leave Polly and Billy by the computer console and cross the long room to the metal door. There is a keypad here, too, and Drug plants himself between me and the door. He's more careful this time and I can't see the numbers he punches in, but my brain records the sound of the four buttons being pushed and I file those away for later replay.

The door slides open, and I follow him into a large chamber.

Chapter 18

All Bets Are Off, Muppit Boy!

There's nothing much here, just ceilings carved out of rough-hewn rock. About twenty yards away I see the nose of a rocket sticking up out of what appears to be a launch tube. The nosecone barely seems large enough to fit one person inside. A conveyer line system with what look like oxygen tanks dangling from it—five canisters in all—sits to one side. There's a hatch open on the nosecone and the conveyer line disappears inside. I stare at those canisters for a moment, my brain replaying everything I already know.

"Those have the microorganisms in them, don't they?"

"Yes, pressurized, and ready to disperse when the rocket reaches a certain altitude. They will be loaded just before launch to avoid accidentally releasing the microorganisms in here." I guess I have a quizzical look on my face because he adds, "There is a place for each canister within the capsule that will control the release."

I try to act cool while recording every detail.

"Did you build this launch pad?"

"No, the military did back in World War II when the Germans started developing missile technology. I merely upgraded it."

Drug holds up his phone, I guess to check the time, because he says, "Your family is being escorted out. Shall we watch?"

He extends one arm toward the door. I glance once more at the rocket and the tanks hanging two feet above me before heading back into the computer room. Drug follows and I hear the door *whoosh* shut behind me. We return to the large monitor where the old couple still waits. I notice that Polly's chainsaw now dangles from a clip on her belt.

"Billy, bring up the surveillance cameras in corridor One-A." Drug watches me, not the monitor.

Billy sets his chainsaw onto a rolling desk chair and bends toward the nearest keyboard.

The launch computer behind me intones, "T-minus twenty minutes and counting."

I have twenty minutes to save the world and I don't have a clue how.

Billy's ancient fingers skitter lithely over the keys and the monitor above my head pops on. It's a color feed of a corridor that looks like all the other ones in this place. Dr. Drug might be an evil genius, but he's no interior decorator.

My family enters the shot and my heart leaps for joy. My mother looks terrified, and I can tell she's crying. Ari supports her. One man with a gun follows behind, looking wary of Ari. Kash and Barn are behind him, and another armed man brings up the rear. Kash is the one they should be worried about. If she sees an opening to kick, those guys will be singing in a boys' choir for the rest of their lives.

"Where are they going?" I don't take my eyes off the screen.

"That metal door just ahead is the west exit," Drug replies matter-of-factly while I watch my entire world leave me behind.

My heart feels heavy enough to pull me right through the floor. But at least my family will be safe.

"A holographic image of a rock cave-in prevents hikers outside from straying too close. Your family will be gassed and then returned to the mainland. I am a man of my word."

I grunt but say nothing. I soak in every detail of these people I love, knowing this might be the last time I see them.

Then something happens so fast I almost miss it. Barney trips, just like he did in the shoe store. He tumbles into the armed man in front of him and knocks that guy into Ari. Ari swings out with a fist and clocks the guy on the jaw, sending the gun clattering to the ground. At the same moment, Kash whirls on the man behind her and kicks him so hard in the privates that *I* wince with pain, even though there's no sound. As Barn clambers to his feet and high fives Kash, Ari grabs for the camera and the image goes black.

Drug makes a gurgling sound of frustration as he depresses a button on the console. "Kill the intruders."

I gasp with horror. "You promised me!"

"All bets are off, Muppit Boy."

I spin around and snatch Billy's chainsaw off the chair. Yanking the cord, I fire the saw to life and swing it around. I thought it would be heavy, but with my newly acquired strength it feels like a plastic lightsaber. I swipe at the phone in Drug's hand.

He leaps back and drops his cell.

Astonishingly, I follow through with the swing and connect the saw blade to the falling phone. Glass shatters and pieces fly everywhere before the destroyed phone flings off to one side of the room. I slam the blade of the saw down onto the computer terminal. Sparks fly as the blade slices through plastic and metal. I raise the saw again and smash the blade down on another part of the terminal, creating a deep cut at least four inches wide.

The lights around me flicker and I know I've done some serious damage, but I don't wait for anyone to react. I yank the saw loose and sprint across the launch headquarters to the door I entered through.

"Stop him!" I hear behind me as I enter the corridor,

followed by the scrambling of people from chairs and Polly's chainsaw roaring to life.

I ignore everything and pelt along the concrete floor, swinging the thunderous chainsaw at anyone who steps close. The overhead fluorescents flicker off and dim emergency lights come on along the upper walls.

A computer voice echoes all around me: "Life support systems have been compromised. Immediate evacuation is recommended."

I did that? Wow! That computer station must be the heart of the complex, I decide, as I keep running.

People spill into the corridor and race past me. A few make tentative grabs, but one wave of the chainsaw and they fall back in a hurry.

As I race along the metallic floor, I'm replaying the footage my brain recorded of the corridors I already went through. That way I make sure not to retrace those steps. I couldn't make out many details on that video feed, so tracking my family might not be easy. On the other hand, this entire place is circular, so I should eventually find the west exit.

Guards enter the corridor and sprint toward me, holding out those dart guns.

I can't let them hit me. They're about fifteen feet away, guns up and ready to fire. I drop to the floor and slide toward them. The darts whizz past above me and the shiny metal floor keeps friction to a minimum. My feet are raised to kick, and the chainsaw is held high.

The men leap to either side so fast it's almost funny.

I slide to a stop and jump to my feet. I actually jump, arching my back and flipping up into a standing position. I'm momentarily amazed at having done something so impossibly athletic, but shove that thought aside. I approach the closer of the fallen men and aim the roaring chainsaw at his head.

"Where's the west exit?"

He points to a corridor off to my left.

I bolt down it. The emergency lights are dim, and I can't see the end of the corridor. I slow my pace in case more goons are waiting to ambush me.

Running footsteps come at me from the darkness at the far end.

I stop the saw and press myself up against the rock wall, in between two lights so the shadows hide me. The footsteps get louder. I leap into the corridor and hold out the chainsaw, one hand on the pull cord.

It's Ari!

I almost collapse with relief.

"Mo!"

Ari has his arms around me before I can even react, lifting both me and the chainsaw off the ground in a bear hug.

I drop the chainsaw and hug my Big Brother harder than I've ever hugged anyone, fighting back tears. "I thought I'd never see you again! Where's Mom?"

He sets me down and I swipe at my eyes.

"Outside on the beach. Come on, Mo."

He snatches up the chainsaw and grabs my hand like he did when I was little. The two of us run into the darkness toward the end of the tunnel.

I notice that a couple of the emergency lights are out, which is why the darkness is so thick. We stop at a metal door and Ari sets the chainsaw down onto the floor. There's a handle that controls a slide bar crossing the width of the door and embedded in the rock walls at each side. He grips the handle and pulls it to the right. The thick steel bar slides aside and stops. Then he grabs the heavy door and pulls it inward.

Echoing through the corridor behind me is that computer voice: "Canister loading to commence in six minutes. Liftoff in zero minus ten minutes."

I freeze as Ari darts out the door.

The rocket's going to launch!

I didn't stop it.

I replay Dr. Drug's words through my brain: *"The rocket controls itself. It's completely automated from an onboard computer, which means once the launch sequence is engaged, no one can stop it."*

Ari spins around when he realizes I'm still inside the bunker.

"Hurry, Mo!"

"Clear the launch area" the computer voice intones. "Repeat, clear the launch area."

"Mo!"

I stare through the door at this man I love more than anyone except my mom. He looks desperate and afraid—I've never seen him this way.

In the distance, I can see the beach. I spot my mom's distinctive bushy hair, Kash's long fish tail braid, and Barn's round face.

I think about all of them enslaved to Dr. Drug for the rest of their lives. I think of all the people who can't afford his antidotes but will have to pay for them anyway or risk not being able to function in our high-tech world. I think of how allergies can lead to other health problems.

I can't let him win!

I focus on Ari and shake my head.

"Mo!"

He starts toward the door.

"I have to stop that rocket!" I shout as I slam the door in his face and fling the handle forward, pushing the bolt back into place.

I hear pounding outside. "Mo! Open the door!"

Tears are streaming down my face. I didn't even know they'd started. "I love you, Ari!"

I scoop up the chainsaw and race back down the corridor.

Chapter 19

I'm Not a Video Game!

The corridors are eerily empty as I run through them. The computer voice alternates between warnings about the failed life support system and the countdown. I notice the air feels stale as I breathe it in, and that can't be good.

I spot no goons and no tech people anywhere as my mind replays the route back to the launch bay and I sprint in that direction. I reach the door to Drug's version of Mission Control without being attacked.

Did everyone evacuate that quickly?

I guess there must've been an escape plan in place, I decide, as I reach out to the keypad on the door. I pause to rewind that footage of Dr. Drug typing in the code and then I replicate it. I note the sounds each button makes and recall the other door into the launch bay.

They're the same! The door opens and I'm in.

Polly stands just inside holding her chainsaw. Dr. Drug waits beside the launch terminal with a cell phone in hand. Otherwise, the room is empty.

"Did you really think I only had one phone?" Drug's voice sounds even more tinny, like maybe the reduced oxygen level is having an effect on him.

I can feel the difference in the air, but it's like my lungs have been so enhanced I think I could breathe at the top of Mount Everest with ease.

The computer voice announces: "Microorganism storage imminent. Liftoff in zero minus eight minutes."

I have to get into that launch bay.

"We're shielded from the launch in here, Muppit Boy," Drug says, holding up the new phone. "So, I intend to have some fun before the oxygen supply is depleted. Kill Polly now."

Polly chirps an exclamation of shock, but then Drug taps the phone and I stiffen.

Like before, I have no control over my body. My left hand pulls hard on the cord, powering my chainsaw into noisy life. Then I run straight at the old woman. I don't want to. I fight my legs for control, but I lose.

She powers up her chainsaw and holds it out like a broadsword. Our blades clash together. The roaring intensifies and I almost lose my grip on the saw handle. She swings down with her saw and I raise mine defensively. The chains clang together again, forcing me back. I think I'm stronger, but she has more experience.

I don't want to hurt her, but I can't stop myself!

"Finish her off, Muppit Boy!" Drug hisses with excitement.

From the corner of my eye, I see him tapping with both thumbs on the phone screen, like he's playing a video game.

Polly gags with fear as I swing around with the saw and slice at her midsection. She leaps back a fraction of a second before my blade swings past. Her billowy dress is caught in the chain and sliced to ribbons, revealing pajamas underneath.

Pajamas?

That momentary distraction frees me for a split second. I note Drug feverishly tapping the screen, but I hesitate before raising the chainsaw and swinging wildly at the old woman. I slam my blade into hers so hard she staggers back. I swing my saw across and smash into hers. It flies from her grasp into the far wall, dropping to the floor and spinning out of control as the chain continues to whirl.

I feel myself moving in for the kill and I can't stop. I'm sweating from the effort, but I can't control my trembling arms. I'm lifting the chainsaw over my head while she cowers in terror.

"Please, Dr. Drug...," she whimpers.

I hear him laugh behind me.

"Out with the old, in with the new. Finish her, Muppit Boy."

My arms start to swing in a downward arc, but I'm resisting, thinking of anything to distract my brain from his programming. That momentary thought about pajamas disrupted his control. If I can think of something longer and more powerful, maybe I can...

Then I have it!

I rewind my brain to my time with Charlie. I experience the joy, the sheer freedom of unconditional love as we rub noses and play catch with the rubber ball. Everything around me vanishes except those images of pure bliss. They overpower my brain and push out everything else, including the commands Drug is sending.

I shift my thoughts slightly, moving the Charlie vids to one side so I can still see the old lady before me. She's cowering in the corner waiting for the deathblow. But it doesn't come because *I* have control again. I turn to face the obviously astonished Dr. Drug, who frantically taps his fingers on the phone screen.

"You will do what I command!"

"I'm *not* a video game!"

I lunge at him and close the gap in two enormous strides, practically leaping across the room. I snatch his phone in my left hand and break it. Then I lift the screaming chainsaw and aim it at his head. I guess even super villains can only take so much because he sprints for the open door like a track star.

I move to follow when the computer voice intones: "Canister loading has commenced."

I stop and watch his billowing cloak disappear into the corridor.

Spinning around, I race to the metal door leading into the launch bay, completely ignoring Polly. She stares at me with her mouth open, while her chainsaw continues its circular dance in the corner. I punch the code into the keypad and the door slides open. Stepping into the bay, I retype the code into the keypad on that side. The door slips shut, and I smash the panel with my fist to keep anyone from getting in.

A motor churns to life and I whirl around to see the line of heavy canisters sliding along the conveyor system toward the open hatch of the nosecone. I consider trying to cut through the mechanism that holds each canister aloft, but the metal chain looks thick and the covering around it even thicker. The canisters hang upside down, I guess because that's how the nozzles fit into a mechanism that will release the microorganisms. I glance at the open hatch. The first canister is almost inside.

I'm out of time.

Raising the screaming chainsaw, I run to the nosecone, taking aim at that closest canister. If I can't stop the tanks from entering the rocket, at least I can keep the microorganisms from getting in. So what if I can't use Wi-Fi ever again? And I hate coffee anyway. I slide to a halt next to the hatch and raise the chainsaw above my head.

"If you do that, Muppit Boy, you will die."

Drug's voice echoes throughout the chamber, and I freeze. The first canister slides past me into the nosecone. The next one is five feet away, but the conveyor moves slowly, I guess to give the mechanism inside time to load each tank.

"What are you talking about?" I call out, not sure where the voice is coming from. "You said these microorganisms won't kill people."

"Ordinary people, no," comes the metallic voice. "But you're no ordinary boy. Combined with the nanites and chemicals I put into your brain, a concentrated dose of these other microorganisms will be lethal."

I suck in a breath of surprise. He could be lying. Probably *is* lying. The second canister looms ever closer. What if he's telling the truth? That means I might die. I think of my family. They're safe. And I think of what that man did to me, how he turned me into a living video game.

I can't let him win.

"Are you willing to die for strangers, Muppit Boy?"

"No, but I am to stop you."

I raise the chainsaw as the next canister approaches.

"Stop being an annoying child and start thinking like a man!"

Whenever some adult tells me I need to think like a man when I'm a long way from *being* a man, I rebel. "Hey, can you see me?"

"Of course, I can see you."

"Good." I swing the chainsaw at the nozzle.

"No!" echoes around me as the nozzle snaps off and the pressurized contents of the canister gush out—right into my face!

Chapter 20

Impossible!

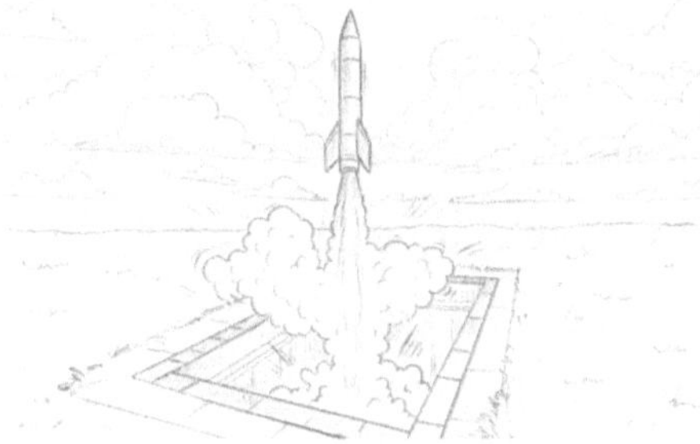

I stagger back, almost pin wheeling, and come close to losing my balance. I'm light-headed and my brain is aflame, like it's a raging coal furnace. My entire body heats up and I struggle a moment to catch my breath.

But I don't die.

In fact, I recover fast, and grin with relief.

"Impossible!"

The word echoes around me, reeking of astonishment.

"You should be dead!"

I ignore him and move to the next canister, this time leaning away as I swipe. The nozzle drops to the floor and rolls away, the contents spewing forth and just missing my face. I end up inhaling the contents anyway, but I guess the direct hit was what made me lightheaded because I don't experience that again. My brain still feels like the inside of an oven, but it doesn't distract me. I move to each of the remaining canisters and release the contents one after the other.

Staggering slightly from the effects of inhaling all those concentrated microorganisms, and with no idea what kind of damage they might have done to me, I stand with the chainsaw still churning and gaze at the empty canisters strewn about my feet. The conveyor line detaches from within the rocket and retracts.

And then I remember.

The first canister went into the nosecone.

I've been so consumed with releasing the microorganisms —and maybe because my brain is confused—that I failed to hear the computer countdown until now.

"T-minus ten seconds and counting."

I spin around quickly, but stagger.

"Nine."

My head swims and I fight to keep from dropping to the floor.

"Eight."

The latch door is sliding shut.

"Seven."

I don't even think; I just run, sprinting across the floor, jumping over the fallen canisters toward that slowly closing door, and then I leap high into the air. I don't know why I do that since I could never jump before, but this time I sail a perfect arc right through the hatchway just before it snaps shut behind me.

I slam down onto hard metal, the chainsaw slipping from my grasp and spinning away as I reach out with both hands to prevent my face from smashing into the floor. Pain shoots through my knees and wrists as I tumble head over heels before crashing into some kind of console.

I should have broken every bone in my body, my feverish brain reminds me, but other than that momentary burst of pain, I'm uninjured.

"Liftoff."

A roaring sound fills the capsule like a tornado and suddenly I'm pinned to the floor, my head jammed at a painful angle against the control console. My stomach drops as I ascend at an alarming rate of speed.

All those rocket videos I watched never prepared me for this! On TV, rockets look like they are rising slowly into the sky. But here, sitting atop the full thrust of the engines beneath me, the pressure almost pulls me right through the floor. The roaring in my ears is so fierce I'm convinced I'll go deaf.

Craning my neck, I look up at where the canister has plugged itself into one of five slots on the opposite side of the small compartment. The other slots are empty because I destroyed those canisters.

I must destroy this one, too!

Will releasing the microorganisms in here be the same as

having them dispersed into the air when the rocket reaches its assigned altitude? I don't think so because the system is likely set up to disperse the chemicals over a wide area, like crop-dusting planes I saw once on a trip to Iowa.

Though I can't even hear it anymore over the roar of the engines, I spot the chainsaw spinning around and around in circles, bumping against the side of the capsule and bouncing off like a dancing top.

The temperature has risen very fast and I'm dripping with sweat. Obviously, this capsule was never intended to carry anyone, so it's not insulated.

I force myself away from the console and drag my body across the floor to the chainsaw. With the intense pressure holding me down, I know I'll only get one good swipe at the canister, and even then, it will take every ounce of strength those nanites can give me.

I reach out, fingers extended, and make a grab for the handle as the chainsaw spins.

I miss.

No!

I stretch out again. The spinning saw makes another complete circle. The handle is almost in my grasp. Anchoring my feet, I push myself forward and feel my fingers slip around the hand grip. I squeeze tight.

Got you!

I roll over onto my back, chainsaw held above me. I study the upside-down canister. There's just enough room where the nozzle fits into the slot for me to swing the saw blade across. If I get it right, I'll sever the nozzle. If I don't, and strike the body of the canister, well, I guess there goes the rocket—and me—in a nice big Fourth of July explosion.

Feeling strength in my core I've never known before, I press upward into a sitting position, despite the G-forces fighting to keep me on the floor. I gaze intently at that nozzle and somehow know exactly how far I need to leap to make contact. I inhale a deep breath and let it out. Then with my free hand I power myself up, scoot my legs underneath me, and dive for the canister, swinging the chainsaw as I do. The blade connects with the nozzle and, with a spray of chemicals, the nozzle separates, and I'm struck in the face by another blast of microorganisms.

I stagger back and slam against the console, the chainsaw swinging backwards over my head. The blade sinks into the control panel and jerks free from my grasp. Sparks erupt all around me and I drop to a crouch, shielding my mass of hair to keep it from catching fire. The chainsaw dances and flips atop the control panel and then spins off to land a foot away from my leg. I reach out and grab the handle, switching it off.

Other than the chain no longer moving, the noise level remains the same. But the sparks above me tell a dangerous tale.

This rocket is seriously wounded.

As though reading my mind, the onboard computer

intones, "System failure. Engines have stalled. Please correct."

Oh, no. That doesn't sound good.

The air is hotter now, and thinner, but I can still breathe with ease. I grip the edge of the console and pull myself up. As I do, the floor beneath my feet slopes sharply downward and I have to hold on to keep from slamming my head into a wall. The acceleration slows and after a few more moments there's no sound but the wind outside rushing past the exterior of the rocket.

Then my world flips upside down!

Only my nanite-enhanced fingers could be strong enough to keep me from flipping over and breaking my neck as the nosecone turns one hundred and eighty degrees. There's no view screen and obviously, no windows, but the twisting feeling in the pit of my stomach tells me all I need to know.

With the thrusters off, the rocket has upended and now plummets downward, out of control!

My heart flies into my throat and panic assails me. I right myself in the now upside-down cabin and rewind my brain to that moment I decided to leap into the rocket.

You didn't really expect to survive, did you?

I guess it was my kid brain in action because I never thought that far ahead. Now I realize there was never any way for me to get out of this alive.

Having no idea how high I am, I don't know if my death

will come in seconds or minutes. I think about Mom and Ari, Kash and Barn. And Charlie. They're the only things I'm leaving behind. That and a lifelong battle with an alter-ego my mother thought was cute. I wonder if I might have been a great detective one day, like Sherlock Holmes. I wonder if Ari will ever marry one of the ladies he's dated. He always told me I'd be his best man if he got married. I wonder who he'll choose now, since I'll be gone.

And then I decide I don't want to die cooped up in this tin can. I surprise myself with that thought because it seems very...grown up. But that's how I feel. I want to die flying, with the sun at my back and the wind in my face.

I rewind my brain to both of my flying episodes with Charlie. Once they are cued up side by side—yes, I can compartmentalize my brain that way—I brace my back against the upside-down control panel and grip the edges with both hands. I lift my legs and aim at the hatch through which I entered. I kick out with all my might.

With a rending and twisting of metal, the hatch door pops out and sails up into the sky out of my view. Cold wind fills the small chamber, chilling me and rushing past the opening at speeds I can't even imagine. I don't know if I'm over land or water, but it doesn't matter. I brace my feet against the base of the console and lean forward into the wind.

I start the replay in my head. I'm one with Charlie, soaring high above San Pedro. I "see" Ari beneath me watching in astonishment. I “see” the ocean beckoning me with its choppy surf and sunlit whitecaps.

I jump through the opening.

Chapter 21

Do You Think He Might Be Contagious?

The rushing wind hits me like a speeding train and drags me up so fast my stomach drops like a sack of rocks. At first, I'm sucked upward alongside the rocket as it plummets, but then wind currents spin my body around and away, allowing the rocket to leave me behind. I'm still high above the ocean, from what I can make out before the whipping wind forces me to snap my eyes shut.

I decide to keep them closed. It's better that way. I soar through the air and feel the flapping of Charlie's wings above me. I'm in Dr. Bell's massive chamber, laughing, heart pounding with joy, as Charlie swoops and ducks and swings me around and around.

I'm happy.

Free fall feels exactly like what it is—free. My head spins, but the images in my brain fill me with delight. I feel myself falling and spinning, while watching myself rising and swooping. It's a disjointed, but amazing sensation.

I almost can't breathe anymore, and I know I'm going to pass out. I try opening my eyes, but I can't. Darkness is all around me, but I'm comforted, not scared, because Charlie is with me. Just before I slip away completely, I feel like I'm rising up and up and up.

I wonder if heaven is real, after all.

Charlie rubs my nose. I feel the gentle pressure of his beak against my skin, that soft, loving caress he always gives me.

Am I dreaming? I must have hit the water by now. Does this mean I'm dead?

I don't see anything but blackness. The gentle rubbing continues, and my eyelids move, fluttering like butterfly wings. They slide upward and light pierces my eyeballs. I blink furiously.

Something floats just above me. I blink once, twice, and suddenly Charlie's face swims into focus. I hear waves striking a shore and feel something gritty on my hands. I lift them and glimpse flecks of wet sand clinging to my fingers.

Where am I?

My brain seems to click on suddenly, like the flipping of a

light switch, and I sit up. I'm on a desolate beach with rocky outcroppings rising behind me in all directions.

Squawk!

I turn to find Charlie regarding me, tilting his head back and forth, and suddenly I understand. I reach out and grab Charlie around his long neck, pulling him in to my shoulder.

"Oh, Charlie, you saved me!"

When I felt myself rising, it was Charlie catching me before I hit the water. That must be the answer!

Charlie pulls back and I release his neck. I guess condors aren't into hugs like dogs are. He regards me with those twirling eyes of his.

"You did save me, didn't you, Charlie?"

He *squawks* and I hear, plain as day in my head, "Yes."

Huh?

"Did you just say yes?"

Squawk.

The word "yes" forms in my mind and I gasp. I can understand him!

He *squawks* a few more times and I blush when I hear, "Love Muppit Boy."

A smile fills my face. "I love you, too, Charlie."

A speedboat rounds the rocky outcropping, and a voice calls out, "Mo!"

It's Ari!

I clamber to my feet and wave my arms with elation. I'm

covered with wet sand from the waves rolling onto the beach, but otherwise I feel strong and healthy.

The boat roars up and slides onto the beach. A beaming Barn is at the tiller and Kash looks more relieved than I've ever seen her. Ari and Mom leap from the boat to sprint across the sand.

Ari scoops me into his arms and once again squeezes me so hard I can't breathe. He sets me down and then it's Mom's turn to crush me, pulling me so close that my face gets lost in her mass of hair.

"I'm okay, Mom," I manage to croak out, but I'm not sure she hears me because she's crying so hard.

I glance sideways at Ari and see him swiping at a tear.

After several long moments where I have to hold my breath because I can't stand the smell of Mom's shampoo, she lets me go and takes the handkerchief Ari holds out, wiping her eyes and staring at me like she'll never let me out of her sight again.

I expect her to say something like, "You have so much explaining to do, mister," like she always does when I make sketchy choices.

But not this time. She finishes wiping her eyes, her lips tremble, and she says, "I love you more than life itself. I hope you know that."

I choke up and feel tears burning my eyes. "I do, Mom."

Ari steps forward. "Come on, Mo, let's get you home."

Before we can even move, a massive, gleaming white

Coast Guard cutter rounds the point and speeds in our direction. It has a wide red stripe slanted downward at the bow and the words U.S. Coast Guard in large black letters painted to the side.

"Uh, I guess the rocket attracted a lot of attention, huh?" I know it's ridiculous to say. Of course, it did!

"Just a little," Ari says with a grin, mimicking my usual sarcasm. "It went down in the ocean a few miles from here."

"Ahoy there," one of the Guard calls out through a bullhorn. She's young, with long hair wafting in the breeze, and looking very snappy in her white uniform. "Is everyone alright?"

"We're fine," Ari calls back.

"We need to take Muppit Boy with us."

I stiffen.

Mom pulls me in. "Why?"

"Oscar Silverman of N.O.S.E."—the Guard stifles a giggle—"needs to debrief him."

Ari steps in front of me. "No one questions my boy without me present."

Mom lets me go and steps up next to Ari. "And me. I'm his mother."

"Not a problem," the young woman calls back. "Stand by for pickup."

Ari hurries to the speedboat and I follow, Mom bringing up the rear. The second I reach the boat, Kash reaches over the side to grab me around the neck. This time my face sinks into her fish tail braid, but I confess her hair smells better than Mom's. If I keep getting these crushing hugs, I might end up with a broken neck.

She pulls back and there's Barn at her side, grinning like he's never been happier.

I grin right back and we high five. "You did that domino thing perfectly, Barn. Took those guys down."

He laughs. "Me being a klutz came in handy for once."

"You're not a klutz," Kash says with a smile. "You're my friend."

He looks slightly embarrassed. "Thanks, Kash." He turns to me. "Did you see the kick she landed on that one dude? He's gonna sound like a little girl for the rest of his life."

We all crack up.

"We make a good team," I say, feeling closer to my friends than ever.

"Yeah, we do," Kash agrees.

"Barn, can you make it back to the mainland?" Ari asks, indicating the speedboat. "Abigail and I are going with Mo."

"Of course," Barn replies with a grin. "I'm a better pilot than my dad."

Kash looks hopeful. "Can't we come with you?"

"Unfortunately, no," Ari says in a mollifying tone. "You heard the guard. They want to debrief Mo."

Kash looks glum. "Okay."

Barn smiles. "You get all the fun, Mo."

"But we get the details later," Kash adds, giving me her "serious" look.

"Of course," I agree, and turn to follow Mom and Ari. Then I remember what I wanted to tell Barn and spin back around. "Oh, and Barn?"

He eyes me expectantly.

"Being your friend never turned me into a loser. It made me the biggest winner ever."

He looks startled, at first, but then I see on his face the understanding that somehow I overheard his conversation with Kash. His round face fills with joy. "Thanks, Mo. Same here."

Mom, Ari, and me step back from the prow of the boat while Barn returns to the engine and restarts it. His parents own a boat and Barn knows sailing inside and out, so I know handling this one is a breeze. The outboard motor roars to life and I watch my friends—no, my family—speed out to sea, skirting the Coast Guard Cutter and vanishing from sight.

In moments, a large, heavy rubber raft is on the beach and we're in it, a male guardsman manning the small motor and speeding us toward the cutter.

Before long, I'm back in Mr. Silverman's office, only this time it's a full house because Dr. Bell is present along with Mom and Ari.

"We tracked the rocket, of course," Silverman tells us, "and located the launch site. My men are searching the bunkers now. I'm sure there won't be anything left worth finding, but it sounds like they had to clear out in a hurry, so maybe we'll get lucky."

I rewind my brain to when I woke up on the island and recite everything I saw and heard. I conclude with Charlie waking me up on the beach. Mom gasps and groans several times during my recitation, and I note Ari gazing at me with a mix of wonder and pride, but I don't stop talking until I've covered every detail.

Dr. Bell "oohs" and "aahs" when I describe what Drug did to me, and about the microorganisms I inhaled that were supposed to poison the world.

Mom plants a hand on my forehead when she hears about the microorganisms—I guess that's a reflex "mom" action.

Bell recommends she not touch me until he's had a chance to perform some examinations.

"Do you think he might be contagious?" Mom looks terrified and a new round of tears blurs her eyes.

"No way to tell without a full exam," Bell says, rubbing his chin with the fingers of his right hand and gazing at me thoughtfully. "We'll have to quarantine him, but he certainly appears healthy enough."

I stare intently at Silverman. "Drug told me he worked

for you, that he invented nanonics and you stole it from him. Is that true?"

"Mo!"

That's Mom, but I keep my eyes on Silverman.

"It's true that his research led to the discovery," Silverman admits, his tone cautionary. "But even then, he was hiding his true identity, and his intentions. Since he worked for N.O.S.E., his research belonged to us. Once we discovered he'd gotten the job under a false identity, he disappeared and was never heard from again. Until he resurfaced as Dr. Drug."

I consider his story. It doesn't match Drug's version, but it sounds reasonable. So how can I know who's telling the truth? Too bad those nanites in my brain aren't lie detectors.

"What about the missing hearing aid?" I ask Silverman. "Do you know what was in it?"

"We were hoping you might."

I shake my head. "Drug never said."

Silverman frowns. "We'll keep searching."

I take a deep breath and let it out. "He changed me. You heard all those things I did. He made me into a *drone*."

The full weight of my "unnaturalness" crashes down on my head like a brick wall and I start to tremble. I focus on Bell. "Can you fix me?"

"I don't know. Maybe you might demonstrate something of your, uh, new abilities for us?" Bell adjusts his glasses and waits.

I spot a fancy metal pen holder on Silverman's desk. "Is that steel?"

"Yes. A gift from my wife."

I eye both men, Silverman seated, and Bell standing behind the large desk. "May I?"

Silverman nods.

I reach out and wrap my fingers around the metal pen holder. It's round like a cup, but fat, so my fingers barely wrap halfway around it. I don't even pull my arm back. I just squeeze with my fingers. The steel snaps and the cup caves in on itself, scattering pens all over the impeccably neat desk.

Silverman flinches back in surprise.

Bell gives a startled intake of breath and stares at me in wonder. "Oh, my! I think it's time we got you into the lab."

Chapter 22

Muppit Boy Saves the World

As soon as I'm rushed into quarantine, another major problem becomes evident – the whole world thinks I'm dead!

Turns out some fisherman grabbed cell phone footage of me falling from the rocket—which looks pretty crazy, I have to admit—but from where his boat was, he didn't see Charlie swoop down and grab me, so the headline all over the media is: "Muppit Boy Dead?"

Silverman had already sent agents to "debrief" Kash and Barn, but the agents were given no instructions related to me "dying" because we didn't know I had! In any case, when reporters descend on Barn and Kash's homes—since everyone knows they're my friends—the agents do the talking, giving a watered-down version of the truth.

They acknowledge a rocket was launched illegally by

person or persons unknown that was allegedly armed with dangerous chemicals. The motive, they say, is undetermined at this time, but they do confirm that Muppit Boy—somehow—stopped the rocket from releasing the chemicals into the atmosphere. When asked about my death, agents at both homes give the same response: "No comment." They refuse to take any further questions, but it's enough for the media to run with, and suddenly, I'm a martyr.

"Muppit Boy Saves the World" is the next headline splashed across the internet, social media, and TV news screens. There's a television in my sealed glass chamber and I watch in astonishment as people call in or tweet their sadness at my death.

People are sad? Why? I've always been a joke, haven't I?

Mom and Ari sit in the quarantine room with me. Bell insisted they wear these ridiculous full body, anti-germ suits, even though they've already touched me and were around me for hours. Mom watches me watch the news, her face behind the visor filled with remorse. Ari grips my hand and squeezes. It feels funny, wrapped up in the plastic suit, but I welcome the love behind that squeeze.

Anderson Cooper of CNN takes calls about my "death." A woman's voice comes through the speaker, and her words are typed out on the screen as Cooper listens.

"I can't believe he's gone."

"Tell us what Muppit Boy meant to you," Cooper says calmly.

There's a pause.

"I loved to laugh at his nose and how he did those clumsy things," the woman's voice replies. "But if you saw me, you'd see I'm no looker, either. Me and my friends, we could relate to Muppit Boy because we're just like him. Somehow, him being so real and, well, so *ordinary*, I guess, made me feel better about *myself*. I know a lot of people who think like that."

Call after call comes in echoing similar sentiments about how I wasn't perfect or beautiful like the usual Reality TV celebrities and how those qualities made me more real, more accessible. They didn't just see a goofy-looking kid running around wearing a red onesie and tripping over things. They saw themselves.

I confess, I'm speechless. I had no idea. I think back on all the people who told me about their favorite episode and wonder how many of them ever got their noses caught in the fridge door or in their mother's hair net. Maybe me doing those things made them feel grateful that their own embarrassments weren't as bad.

I look over at Mom, my mouth hanging open, and then mute the TV with the remote. "Did you know people felt that way?"

She nods. "I got a lot of rude comments about your nose, but those I deleted. Most were like these. They talked about how much you helped them, or their kids, feel good about their own imperfections."

"Why didn't you ever tell me?"

"I thought you were too young to understand. And when you came to me two years ago and begged me to stop putting you on the show, I finally understood how much it all hurt you. Unfortunately, while I removed the most embarrassing videos from my channel, I couldn't erase them from the Net." She pauses and looks down, I guess collecting her thoughts. "What that man said about me—"

"Mom."

She holds up a heavily gloved hand. "I need to finish, Mo, just like you need to finish when you're recounting a rewind."

I close my mouth and listen.

"Everything he said was true, honey. I did use you, despite criticizing parents on the show for exploiting *their* kids for attention or profit. I'm guilty of both. I was lonely after your dad died and YouTube made me feel connected to other people. And I guess I told myself you were having fun. When you finally admitted how miserable you were, how other kids mocked you, it broke my heart. I never wanted to hurt you, Mo. I hope you believe that. I just got caught up in the attention trap."

My mouth is dry and I'm not sure I can speak. I look at Ari, but he says nothing. He understands this is between Mom and me.

I clear my throat awkwardly. "It's okay, Mom. I think maybe, well maybe it was a good thing you did. All these people"—I point at the muted TV screen—"are proof of that."

Her eyes widen and she looks stunned for a moment. And then she smiles. "My little boy isn't a little boy anymore."

I'm not sure why, but that makes me feel good.

To quell all the "Muppit Boy is Dead" talk, Silverman agrees to let Mom do an episode of her show from the medical wing so the public can see that I'm alive and well but undergoing examinations to make sure no radiation from the rocket contaminated me. It sounds like a good story and since no reporters are allowed in to ask any questions, it works.

For the next few days, "Muppit Boy Lives" is the top story, along with my heroics in stopping the rocket and the still-unknown chemicals that might have been unleashed into the atmosphere. Silverman doesn't speak to the media, but his superiors at Homeland Security fill in some of the gaps regarding the incident and they praise my "clear-headed thinking" that saved millions from a potentially dire fate.

Overnight, Muppit Boy isn't a dorky kid with a big nose anymore. Suddenly, he's a hero who saved the world. I guess it might have been fun to bask in all the positive attention for a change, but unfortunately quarantine doesn't allow for that. However, I experience an unaccustomed pride in myself as I watch the coverage. Between the accolades and the support from people young and old, I no longer disdain the character my mother created.

I am, for now and always, Muppit Boy, and proud to be so.

Okay, I've been cooped up in this hospital wing for over three weeks and I'm close to going supernova! Seriously, if it weren't for my daily—limited because of my quarantine status—play sessions with Charlie, and visits from Mom and Ari, I'd lose my mind!

I've had every test that can be done on a human being and Bell is still no closer to understanding everything about me that's been "altered." Yes, my blood, muscles, and bones are infused with nanites. Since Bell doesn't know what chemicals Drug injected into me in addition to the nanites, he doesn't know what effect they might have long term. We run tests for chocolate, coffee, and Wi-Fi allergies and I don't have any of them.

What's particularly odd is that I seem to be perfectly healthy, inside and out. Despite everything I went through, I sustained no physical injuries, not even any cuts or bruises. And get this—my lifelong allergy to pollen is gone! Bell tests me with several different kinds of pollen and I have no reaction. Somehow, whatever Drug did to me has resulted in a body devoid of defects.

Except my nose, of course.

And my ADHD.

But at least I no longer need glasses. Vision is twenty-twenty. I haven't had that, well, ever, I don't think.

The other weird development—and my favorite—is my ability to communicate with Charlie. Bell isn't sure, but he thinks it's the nanites in our brains transmitting our feelings and turning them into words. Whatever the reason, I feel closer to Charlie than ever.

I miss Kash and Barn, though. I desperately want to see them, especially now that Bell has removed me from quarantine, but Silverman nixes the idea.

"You'll see them when you go home. Best for us not to have too many people visiting this facility."

I understand but am not happy about it.

Bell also puts me through a huge number of physical tests —strength, running, jumping. I continually stun myself with how strong and fast I am now, and how coordinated! I can even jump fifteen feet into the air, straight up. As Charlie soars overhead, I leap upwards, and he snatches hold of my arms. We've become an amazing team now that we can think the same thoughts and feel the same feelings. It's like he's an extension of me and me of him. I think Mom is a little jealous, but Ari says it's cool.

Finally, after four weeks, Bell and Silverman agree to let me go home. I'm so stunned I can't speak for a long moment.

"But what all have you learned?" I know about the stuff that makes me stronger than a grown man, but I want to know how my brain has been affected.

Bell and Silverman exchange a look that troubles me. They're hiding something.

"We need to correlate all the data, Mo," Bell says, his tone cagey.

He may be a brilliant scientist, but he's a lousy liar.

"We'll let you know in a few days."

"In the meantime," Silverman jumps in before I can speak, "go home and bask in the glory you've earned. Just remember our debriefing and stick to the 'public' version of the story."

I know these men too well by now, and there's something they're not telling me, something I'm not going to like.

Chapter 23

What's Wrong?

The first sign that something's wrong is when I walk into my house to find Kash and Barn waiting to hug me and slap me on the back and gush over how much they missed me. The funny part is how they talk over each other and even correct each other, launching into mini-arguments that are meaningless and go nowhere. It's like they've become best buds in my absence and I'm the third wheel.

I take it back. That's not funny.

What's *disturbing* is how much taller both of them have gotten in the month since I saw them last. Seriously, I feel like an elementary school kid next to them, and waves of anxiety sweep over me as I recall how Silverman and Bell looked when they sent me off with Mom and Ari.

But I'm so happy to see my friends that the feeling of

discomfort wears off right away. While we have dinner, they talk over each other, recounting stories about St. Mary's and how I'm the main topic of conversation.

After we eat, Mom brings out a "welcome home" cake. I try not to laugh at the chocolate frosting, but Mom winks at me as she sets it onto the table, so I know she did it on purpose.

The following day at school is particularly weird. The repairs have been completed and we're back to the regular schedule in our classrooms. Ari walks to school with me, Kash, and Barn. I'm swamped as I enter the parking lot. The press got wind of my return and are camped out in front of St. Mary's, swooping in like vultures the moment they see me.

I answer some of the reporters' questions, while kids who've never talked to me hover excitedly nearby, but I stick with the story already released and, naturally, give no hint of my "enhanced" abilities. I'll have to be super careful not to reveal those by accident. That means I can't throw dirtbags like Mason Rizzo through walls, much as I'd like to.

When asked by kids and teachers about my missing glasses, I reply, "Contact lenses."

I'm happy to see Sister Ella and sit in her science class once again. I find my eyes drawn to the box of old eyeglasses and used hearing aids on her desk. She's been collecting them all year to send to needy kids in other countries.

I'm sure they've been scanned and thoroughly checked out by Silverman's people, but I keep wondering what happened to the aid the old people were looking for, and exactly what microorganisms were in that aid. And why did Sammy break in here in the first place? Silverman suspects it was chemicals Sister Ella kept in the room for experiments, but I'm not so sure. Even Silverman admits that Bell's "opinion" of Sammy's drug sniffing abilities is highly inflated.

As I search the cafeteria for Barn and Kash, I answer question after question from kids who used to make fun of me or ignore me completely. I was a super famous joke and now I'm a super famous hero. But I'm the same kid (just a little, you know, improved.) Deep down, where it counts, I'm the same. Somehow, in everyone's eyes who didn't think so before, I'm now someone worth talking to. I'm polite to these kids, but my gaze roams the cafeteria for my *real* friends. I spot them at a corner table and zig zag through milling people in that direction.

My path is suddenly blocked by Mason Rizzo. I shiver with disquiet at how much taller he's gotten. At least an inch, which means he's now three inches taller than me. I know I can pick him up and toss him across the room, despite his bigger muscles, but I can't allow that to happen.

"What do you want, Rizzo?"

I keep my voice steady and serious. I don't want trouble. I

see Kash stand up behind him and start toward us. I catch her eye and shake my head slightly.

Rizzo stares at me like he's trying to figure out if he recognizes me. "You really did all that, with the rocket and stuff? I mean, it was on the news, but..." He trails off, looking lost for words, a decidedly un-Rizzo-like behavior.

"Yep," I reply, keeping my face neutral. "Me and my big nose."

I realize the cafeteria has fallen silent. From the corner of my eye, I spot the principal making her way toward us, I guess because she thinks we're going to fight.

But Rizzo doesn't throw a punch. Instead, he grins, almost like we're friends. "You're not the worthless dweeb I thought you were."

He raises a fist.

I blink a moment before realizing what he wants and then I bump his fist with mine. He moves off through the crowd and I find myself staring at Kash and Barn. They shrug, and I happily join them.

A few days after my return home, I'm down in my room playing a game on my computer when there's a knock at the door.

"Come on in."

I look up the stairs and see Mom standing at the top. Even in the shadowy lighting, I know something's wrong.

"You have company, Mo."

I watch as Mom descends the stairs, followed by Ari, Mr. Silverman, and Dr. Bell. They all look like they just came from a funeral. I feel invisible as they gather around and look at everything in the room but my face.

"What's wrong?"

"We've reached some conclusions, Mo," Silverman says, but even he has trouble making eye contact. He stops and glances at Bell.

The little man shifts nervously from foot to foot. "I've analyzed all the data and run it by the best people we have and, well, everyone is in agreement."

My body feels like it's tied into knots. "What's wrong?"

Everyone watches Bell.

He clears his throat. "Well, um, your pituitary gland has, somehow, shrunk."

"What does the pituitary gland do?"

"Well, it sits here." He points to the area just above his nose between his eyes. "The pituitary makes important hormones, like growth and puberty, that are essential to physical development."

I'm feeling colder by the second. "So, what's wrong with mine?"

"It's, well, it's abnormally small, and it's not... functioning," Bell replies, his voice slightly unsteady.

"What does that mean?" I'm picturing Barn and Kash and Rizzo so much taller than me.

"Your body isn't producing any of those hormones, Mo," Ari says when Bell hesitates. "They tried giving you growth hormone during your stay at the institute, but your body rejected it. Same with puberty hormones."

I'm not liking any of this and I'm scared, so of course I resort to sarcasm. "So, what are you saying? I'll be in middle school forever?" I try for a laugh, but none of them join me.

"Not middle school, no," Silverman says, with a glance at Mom.

She lifts her head and I see wetness around her eyes. "Remember how your favorite character as a child was Peter Pan? You had me read that book over and over again."

My mouth drops open as I suddenly understand what they're *not* saying. "I'm going to stay twelve?"

The silence around me is so heavy I could wear it as a winter coat.

Ari clears his throat. "Uh, that's how it looks right now, Mo." His eyes are glistening, and his face is twisted up, like he's fighting back some great pain.

"That's crazy!" I leap to my feet.

"We're still searching for a solution," Bell says quickly, like I might punch him or something. "We think it has to do with the concentrated infusion of microorganisms you inhaled when you destroyed those canisters, but without the exact makeup and concentration you experienced, we can't be certain. I won't give up until I have an answer."

"But in the meantime...," Silverman eyes me with sympathy.

"I can't stay twelve!" My brain is overloading again and I'm keenly aware of my high, "little boy" voice. "I can't! It's the worst age ever!"

"Peter Pan did," Mom offers, and I know she's trying to be helpful, but that's not what I want to hear.

"Peter Pan *wanted* to stay a child," I retort, my brain spinning. "He could've grown up if he left Neverland, but he didn't *want* to. I want to!"

Ari is there, on his knees, hands on both of my shoulders, squeezing gently. "Breathe, Mo."

I look up at him and see anguish on his face. And love. I breathe in and out and fight to process this impossible news. "But Ari..." I can't go on. My voice croaks and I feel like I'm breaking in two.

"Mo, who's my boy?"

Tears force their way out and I don't try to stop them. "Me. But that's the problem. I'll *always* be your boy. I'll never be your teen or your college graduate. I'll never be your best man because I'll never *be* a man."

He squeezes my shoulders again. "Mo, right here, right now, you're the best man I know. If and when I get married, you *will* stand by my side."

I nod as tears dribble down my cheeks. "But you can

never be that for me. I know why Peter Pan didn't wanna grow up. He didn't have someone like you showing him how to be a man. I wanted to make you proud, Ari, by being the kind of father to my kids that you are to me. I'll never get to do that now."

"Oh, Mo." He looks as broken as I feel.

I search his eyes through my tears. "Did you mean what you said to that Coast Guard lady about me being your boy?"

He looks slightly embarrassed. "I know I don't have the right, but I do think of you like a son."

I throw my arms around him and cry into his jacket. My whole life has been a joke and now I find the joke's on me. What did I ever do to deserve this?

Ari stays with me while Mom escorts the others out. Then she comes back downstairs and stares at me, still cradled in Ari's arms.

"I'd like to be alone now," I finally say, when I can control my voice.

"Mo...." That's Mom, but I don't look at her.

"We're here for you, Mo," Ari says.

I don't respond and they leave the room. I plop down onto my bed and cry myself to sleep.

Chapter 24

I Need A Partner

I don't return to St. Mary's. There's only two weeks left and I can't face anyone. I don't even want to see Kash and Barn, though they come over every day anyway. And every day they look taller than me. That's probably my imagination at work, but it unnerves me to the point that I hope they stop coming. They know about my "condition," but I don't think it's really sunk in that they will grow up and leave me behind.

I think about nothing else.

Ari comes every day, too, and offers to take me out for some fun. But I just want to hide away and let the world forget about me. How much longer can I go out in public anyway without people starting to notice I'm not growing? I'm one of the most famous people in the world and everyone knows me. Questions will be raised, questions me and Mom can't answer without lying. And what kind of lie could cover up something like this, anyway?

There's a pointless celebration for my "thirteenth" birthday in June, but at least my mom doesn't put thirteen candles on the cake. I can't help my sarcasm when I snarl, "You'll save tons of money on my birthdays, Mom. You can use the same twelve candles forever."

She looks hurt and I know she's having a really hard time with this, but I just feel like somebody threw me under a steamroller and it keeps crushing me over and over again. Barn and Kash are there, of course, and they try hard to cheer me up, but as soon as I finish opening my gifts—which include the latest PlayStation—I excuse myself and retreat to my room.

Alone.

That's how I pass my days, now—alone—and that's how I want to *keep* passing them. Even Mom and Ari, though they try not to, look at me with sympathy, and I know they're seeing my lack of growth. So do I, every time I look in the mirror.

The only thing that ever looks bigger is my nose.

A week after my birthday, Ari comes over with Silverman and Bell. Mom lets them into my room where I sit at my desk, playing solitaire on the computer. Silverman carries an enormous box that he sets on my bed.

"What's that?"

"A birthday present," Silverman replies evenly. "I'll let Ari explain."

Everyone seems to talk around me, like they're walking barefoot across hot coals.

"First off, Mo," Ari begins, awkward and cautious. "We've decided you won't be going back to school in the fall."

That catches my attention and I glance at Mom.

She nods.

"Given your...situation, too many questions might be raised in the coming year," Bell puts in, adjusting his glasses. "Boys your age typically have major growth spurts and, well, you understand."

I don't really care. At school, I'd just feel like I'm a freak in a zoo, even though the other kids won't know I'm a freak. At least, not right away. But *I'd* know and that's what matters.

I study Ari's clothing. He wears his jacket and pants, but no tie, and sports a topcoat, something I've never seen before.

He must notice my staring because he says, "I don't work for the LAPD anymore."

My breath hitches in my throat. "Why didn't you tell me?"

"I just did. I work for Oscar now." He indicates Silverman.

"You work for N.O.S.E.?"

"Yes, as an agent. And the thing is, Mo, I need a partner. Since you can't go back to school, how'd you like to work with me?"

My eyes practically fall out of their sockets. "Work with you? Every day?"

"Every day. You can put that amazing brain of yours to the use it was made for."

I break into a huge smile, and then the smile falters. "I can't. Everybody knows Muppit Boy. They'll see I'm not growing."

Ari smiles. "Only if they recognize you."

"I don't get it. You want me to wear a disguise, like a fake mustache and beard? I don't think that'll wash."

Silverman steps forward and gazes at me with more respect than any adult ever has, except Ari. "Mo, you are one of the bravest, most resourceful people I've ever met. With your enhanced nanonic abilities, you can be a major asset to N.O.S.E. And, quite frankly, Charlie refuses to work with anyone else. I'd like you to work for me, as an agent, with pay. You, Ari, and Charlie will be a team, ferreting out some of the more unusual threats to our country. What do you say?"

I'm stunned, and of *course*, I want to say yes. What kid wouldn't? It's seriously the chance of a lifetime. But I pause and look at Mom. "Mom? Is it okay with you? I *am* still twelve, after all."

Mom looks equal parts proud and scared. "I'll worry about you getting hurt, but I know Ari will protect you."

"More like the other way around, Abigail," Ari says with a chuckle.

"I want you to be happy, Mo," Mom adds with a sad smile.

Would working with Ari and Charlie make me happy, despite my permanent status as a twelve-year-old? Is Muppit Boy snarky?

"Yes," I say to Silverman and Ari. "Yes, I wanna work with you guys."

With a huge grin on his face, Ari claps me on the shoulder.

Then reality hits.

"But how are we gonna keep people from recognizing Muppit Boy?"

"That's where this comes in," Silverman says, bending to retrieve the large box from my bed. He sets it down on my desk.

"Open it, Mo," Ari says.

I slip the top off the box and stare uncomprehendingly at what looks like a green and brown Halloween costume. Setting the lid aside, I pull up the part of the costume I surmise would go over my chest and see faux feathers covering the entire thing. In the upper center, between an outline of muscular pecs I'll never have in real life, is a kind of logo. It looks like Charlie's wings spread open. At the center of the wings are the letters "CK."

"A bird costume?"

"A condor costume," Bell says, sounding very smug.

"Oh, I stand corrected," I sneer. "A *condor* costume. I'll look real professional walking around in a condor onesie!"

"Who said anything about walking?"

That's Ari, and I gaze at him quizzically.

"Look under the costume, Mo."

I pull out the rest of the onesie—which is really a *threesie* since the outfit is in three pieces—and extract a full head-covering that looks a lot like Charlie, big nose and all.

"Great. My nose will be even bigger."

"Keep looking," Ari urges.

I set the mask and costume onto my desk and pull out the tissue paper covering something else. My heart nearly stops as I behold a gorgeous set of wings, each one easily six feet long, which explains the length of the box. Faux feathers matching the colors of Charlie's wings cover a metallic frame that looks solid enough to hoist a cow.

I spin around and face everyone, breaths coming in short bursts. "Are you saying...I can fly?"

Silverman chuckles. "Yes, Mo, that's what we're saying."

Bell flashes a proud grin. "They have nanites in them that we cultivated from the ones inside you. Once strapped on, those wings will respond directly to your brainwaves—like Bluetooth, if you will. Just as you do with your arms and legs, all you have to do is think what you want the wings to do, and they'll respond as though they're part of your body."

My mouth hangs open and I stare at him. My brain fights to process this information overload and I'm afraid it'll slide off the table any moment. I turn to Ari.

"It's true, Mo. You're already something of a superhero and superheroes wear costumes to disguise their identity. This way no one will recognize you."

I'm so excited I forget to breathe for a moment. "Uh, what's the 'CK' stand for?"

"Condor Kid," Bell says proudly.

"Condor Kid?"

"It was Charlie's idea," Bell adds solemnly. "And I didn't want to make him mad."

Suddenly, "Condor Kid" doesn't sound so bad.

I pick up the mask and study it a moment. Yeah, condors are pretty unattractive. Fits me perfectly. I feel every set of eyes boring into me and I sense the hope behind them, the hope that I can find happiness despite my circumstances. And I think I can, at least for now.

I eye Ari mischievously. "So, when do I learn how to fly?"

He grins, and I return it.

I don't know what the future holds for Muppit Boy, Condor Kid, or even Peter Pan.

But I'm ready to find out.

THE END

Muppit Boy (and Condor Kid) Will Return in
MUPPIT BOY AND THE WHEEL OF POWER

Preview after Author Bio

About the Author

Michael J. Bowler is the award-winning author of the teen and young adult novels A MATTER OF TIME, THE LANCE CHRONICLES, THE HEALER CHRONICLES, THE FILM MILIEU THRILLER SERIES, THE INVICTUS CHRONICLES, and FOREVER BOY.

LOSING AUSTIN is suitable for readers twelve and up.

His screenplay, "THE GOD MACHINE," won First Place in the 2017 Scriptapalooza competition and in the 2023 Tarzana International Film Festival.

He grew up in San Rafael, California. He worked as producer, writer, and/or director on several ultra-low-budget horror films, including "Hell Spa," "Fatal Images," "Club Dead," and "Things II."

He taught high school in Hawthorne, California—both in general education and to students with learning disabilities—in subjects ranging from English and Strength Training to Algebra, Biology, and Yearbook.

He has been a volunteer Big Brother to eight different boys with the Catholic Big Brothers Big Sisters program, a decades-long volunteer within the juvenile justice system in Los Angeles and is a single dad to an adopted child. He has been honored as Probation Volunteer of the Year, YMCA Volunteer of the Year, California Big Brother of the Year, and National Big Brother of the Year. The "National" honor allowed him and three of his Little Brothers to visit the White House and meet the president in the Oval Office.

Website: michaeljbowler.com
FB: michaeljbowlerauthor
X: @MichaelJBowler
Instagram: @michaeljbowler
YouTube: https://www.youtube.com/channel/UC2NXCPry4DDgJZOVDUxVtMw

Join my mailing list at MichaelJBowler.com for updates on upcoming releases and free reads.

More Muppit Boy Coming Soon

MUPPIT BOY AND THE WHEEL OF POWER

CHAPTER ONE
I'm Condor Kid

My name is Mo Fitzroy, I'm perpetually twelve years old (more on that later), my best animal friend is a California

Condor, and I'm *finally* enjoying some summer fun with my two best human friends, Barney and Kashvi, after surviving a grueling six weeks of what can best be described as "superhero boot camp."

Am I a superhero? The world sort-of thinks of me that way as *Muppit Boy* (my childhood alter ego created by my mom on her YouTube channel) because I saved the world (sort of) from a major germ attack launched by an evil genius called Dr. Drug. He escaped, and I'm sure I'll battle him again someday.

Right now, we're at one of those traveling carnivals that's set up near the beach here in San Pedro, so I have a great view of the Pacific Ocean on this warm summer day. I'm having a blast on the rides, but the place is packed with people, and *everyone* knows who I am, so I've been greeted with "Welcome home, Muppit Boy!" and "Where have you been all summer?" literally the whole day!

I try to be polite to everyone and realize even more than before that fame is a double-edged sword. I really just want to have fun with my friends, but I also understand why people are interested in me. My mom says that's just me growing up, that I understand these things. If only I *could* grow up.

Of course, I see tons of kids from my school, most of whom mocked me before my heroics of the previous spring, all playing nice now and pretending to be my friend. Just days before that story broke these same kids made fun of my nose.

"Ignore them, Mo," Kash keeps saying, but that's not easy to do.

I'm wearing the biggest pair of sunglasses I could find that practically cover my whole face, but my most prominent facial feature gives me away – my larger than average nose. If I've heard one nose joke, I've heard them all and my self-esteem always teeters on the edge of a steep cliff, ready to plunge downward at the next cutting remark.

Kashvi is a pretty Indian girl who wears her long black hair in a single fishtail braid and excels at martial arts. Barney has been my best friend since first grade, and we talk about everything. At least, we used to. Now that I've been gone so long, he and Kash are more buddy buddy than ever. Barn is the opposite of athletic, chubby with a round face and a penchant for being super clumsy. His red hair gleams in the bright sunlight as we wander through the midway looking for a game to play.

It feels like every eye in the place follows me as I walk. I might just be paranoid, but I'm sure it's because I've stopped growing and look like a small twelve-year-old instead of my actual age, which is thirteen but thanks to Dr. Drug my body development is frozen at twelve and won't budge.

Crazy, huh?

Kash and Barn are both much taller than me now and I hate that. At the Air Force Base where I had my boot camp, I got to wear my new superhero costume most of the time, so I felt less self-conscious about my height and my nose. But out here, back in the town where I grew up, I stand out like a sore thumb.

Barn and Kash know that I'm not growing anymore, but they don't know that I have super strength and super speed or that I can fly. And I'm not allowed to tell them. I now work for a top-secret government agency called (unfortunately) N.O.S.E alongside my awesome Big Brother mentor, Ari, and a super-powered condor named Charlie. It's because of Charlie that I have a condor costume to hide my identity.

I *so* wish I could tell my best friends, but Oscar—the guy I work for—says it would put them in too much danger. I guess I know that from superhero movies and comics, but I still feel like I'm lying to my friends. My mom knows everything, of course, but no one else.

I've been made fun of most of my life for embarrassing videos as Muppit Boy on my mom's channel, so it would be kind of nice to finally be known for doing something positive. Sure, the Dr. Drug incident has elevated my cred a lot, but how long before people forget and go back to laughing about my nose or notice that I'm not growing?

I try to shake off these feelings as I watch Kash throw darts at balloons tacked to the back wall of an arcade booth. She scores a win and is handed what looks like a stuffed anteater. She tosses off a bright smile and shrugs.

"You can give that to your little cousin," Barn says, eyeing the ugly stuffy with revulsion. "Little kids like stuffies."

"What do you think, Mo?" She holds the hideous thing in front of me as we jostle our way through the crowd.

I grimace. "I think it'll give your cousin nightmares."

She laughs.

"Let's go on more rides, Mo," Barn says, tossing an empty candy wrapper into a trash can.

"Sure," I say, though the long waits in line have been challenging because everyone wants me to talk about how I saved the world. Of course, I can't tell the full truth and must stick to the official version Oscar created, but I still feel some pride in myself for what I *can* share.

At least until I hear a voice shout, "Look, it's Muppit Boy and his nose!"

My temper flares and I spin around to find Julian Briggs standing at the entrance to the midway smirking at me. He's tall and athletic. Next to him is Mason Rizzo, the buff bully who's made my life hell the past few years. The third wheel of their crew isn't around today.

"Shut your mouth, Briggs!" Kash growls beside me.

I'm about to shoot out a snarky response when I'm stunned to see Rizzo scowl at his friend. "Shut up, Julian. Let's go."

Briggs' face collapses in shock. Rizzo eyes me across the expanse of the midway and then turns to go the opposite way. Shocked, Briggs follows him.

"That was weird," Barn says, watching them walk away. "I never knew Rizzo to not make fun of us."

"Me either." I can't imagine what's going on with the bane of my existence, but at least I avoided a confrontation. Despite Rizzo beating me on the muscles front, the nanites Dr. Drug put into my body give me more than enough strength to throw him across this entire midway with ease.

"Let's go on the Ferris wheel," Kash suggests.

I turn to where she points. An enormously high Ferris wheel stands off in the distance doing a slow spin as it off-loads and on-loads passengers into gondolas that seat four people each. It's not a crazy fast ride like the Zipper and I'll be in a gondola with just my friends, so no one else can intrude. That's what I need right now.

"Sounds like a plan. Barn?"

Barney is attempting to tie his shoelaces and losing the battle. Sighing heavily, Kash drops to a squat and expertly ties them into a double bow. Barn offers her a shy smile, and we leave the midway, pressing through the crowd toward the massive wheel just ahead.

As we walk, I fidget and squirm because of the costume under my clothes. So far, the world hasn't met my new alter ego, but I wear the entire outfit under my clothes in case of emergency. Oscar and Ari never said I couldn't, so why not? I'll tell you why not. It's eighty degrees out and I'm dying under all these clothes! Most everyone wears short pants and a tee shirt or tank top.

Me, I wear an extra-large hoodie to cover the folded wings on my back and long sweats to cover the lower half of the costume. The costume doesn't require boots, so I wear my new sneakers to complete the ensemble. The folded wings were invented by Dr. Rudy Bell, who works with Oscar, and, despite them each being six feet long when extended, they fold so compactly that I honestly don't feel them against the middle of my back.

But the heat kills me and sweat dribbles down my forehead onto my nose. No jokes, please. I wipe away the sweat and stop. Surprised, my friends stop too.

"What's up, Mo?" Kash asks, her features scrunched with worry.

I stare at the crowd waiting to board the Ferris wheel and shake my head. "Too many people. You guys get in line. I'm gonna hide out in the bathroom. My brain is sliding a bit."

I have ADHD, which may or may not have helped my brain move faster with the infusion of nanites, but when there's tons of sensory overload, like right now, I feel like it'll slide off the table completely.

Kash looks disappointed, but Barn understands. "It's cool, Mo. We'll meet up after the ride. C'mon, Kash."

Kash studies me with concern. "You okay? Wanna drink or something?"

"Naw, just a few minutes of peace and quiet." And I mean that.

She nods and gives Barn a playful shove. "Well, let's get going."

They vanish into the crowd. I find the nearest boys' bathroom and duck inside without being seen. Thankfully, the urinals are free and all the stall doors ajar. I dart into the stall farthest from the entrance and lock the door. Then I climb up onto the closed toilet seat and squat, allowing the peace and quiet to fill me.

Concentrating on being calm is difficult with the smell of pee all around me, but I tune that out and focus, just like Ari has always taught me.

I don't know how long I've been meditating when I hear youthful voices enter the bathroom.

"I was just getting started with Muppit Boy, Mason. Why'd you stop me?"

That voice belongs to Julian Briggs. I'd know it anywhere, except maybe it's getting deeper?

"Haven't you thought about all that stuff on the news about him?" Rizzo replies.

"So what?" Briggs replies. "You know they make that stuff up."

"Maybe." He pauses and I hear them both peeing. A zipper is tightened. "I got more muscles than that twerp any day, but how'd he do all that stuff?"

"I told you, it's fake."

"What if it's not? You brave enough to hide in a rocket just to save people you don't know?"

"Course."

"Yeah, right."

Pounding footsteps enter the bathroom. "Mason! There you are."

"What's up, Lorenzo?"

"The Ferris wheel is falling! Come on or you'll miss it!"

Three sets of feet stomp out of the bathroom. I hear people in the park screaming. The Ferris wheel is falling? How can that happen and how many people will be hurt or killed?

I have to help!

I leap off the toilet bowl and yank my hoodie up and over my head. The head piece for my costume dangles from a string around my neck. I pull it loose even as I'm kicking off my shoes and shucking off my sweats. I slide my feet back into my sneakers and consider the mask. It's soft and pulls over my head. It looks mostly orange with splashes of purple. The eye holes are more in front than on a real condor, but the sharp hooked beak looks like the real deal. It has mini speakers on the inside that go over the ears so I can use my phone.

I grab my phone from the sweatpants and slide it into the pocket built into the costume pants, which look like the body of a condor with faux feathers attached.

I think about my wings moving and feel them stir against my back. They're ready for flight. Listening, I can tell the bathroom is empty and no one is nearby outside so I unlatch the stall door and step out. I scoop up my clothes and dash to a scratched mirror. The front of my costume shows muscular pecs I don't have, and more faux feathers are all over my torso. In the center of my chest is a logo – large spreading wings with CK in the center.

More screams assail my ears, and I wait no longer. Slipping the mask over my head, I make sure the eye holes are in place and the fit is snug before bolting outside. I stuff my clothes between the corner of the bathroom and a tree resting up against it. Then I look out over the crowd.

The enormous Ferris wheel has stopped turning and tilts to one side at a dangerous angle. From what I can see, the ride looks full. People are screaming in terror. Are Kash and Barn in one of those gondolas? It doesn't matter. It's up to me to save them all.

"Who are you?"

I glance down at a small boy holding pink cotton candy in one hand and staring at me in wonder.

I don't hesitate. "I'm Condor Kid." I will my wings to open and they unfurl to their full six-foot length behind me, causing the boy to lurch back in fear. In the "Batman" voice I spent so much time perfecting during boot camp, I say, "Don't worry, kid. I'm a superhero."

Then I leap into the air, and my wings take over, flapping wildly, sending me soaring up and over the astonished crowd and hurtling toward the toppling Ferris wheel.

Check Out Losing Austin

If you liked this book, you might enjoy another by Michael J. Bowler entitled *Losing Austin.* It's suitable for ages 12-13 and up.

I made my big brother disappear. Not like a magician makes an elephant disappear, but I *did* drive him away, and he *did* disappear. Did I murder him like everyone thought? No. But since he vanished into thin air, he could have been killed and if he had been, it would've been my fault, but.... I'll explain—even though no one will believe me because, honestly, making elephants disappear is easier to accept than what happened to my brother.

We lived in a town called Mill Valley in Northern California. My expansive, two-story home sat atop Mount Tamalpais, right near the Panoramic Highway that overlooked a mountainside covered with tall, ageless trees and a really amazing view of the Pacific Ocean. At least, that's what my parents kept saying. They took me and Austin on hikes into the woods when we were younger, but by the time I got to middle school, Mom only took Austin because I refused to go. Hiking wasn't my thing, and I didn't give a rip about nature. Seen one tree, seen 'em all.

My house was made of redwood, with tons of windows and a huge backyard. It looked beautiful from the highway, though I didn't much notice that until I started getting better at drawing. But I always loved the pool and used it a lot during the summer.

Like most boys my age, I loved video games back then. That was my *thing*. School bored me, despite my parents gushing over how *wonderful* Mill Valley schools were and how I'd go on to some big university someday. Did they ever ask me what I wanted? Oh, hell, no! By the time I'd turned twelve, I knew what I wanted to do—design graphics for video games. I could draw. So could my older brother. Adults said it was genetic because our dad was an architect and all. A gift, they said. Whatever the reason, we could create almost anything with just a pencil and paper.

But, and here's the *big* but—my brother was "different." All the doctors said Austin presented "autism-like" aspects, but none would officially diagnose him as being on the spectrum. His uniqueness sent them scrambling for their medical journals to research similar cases, and they did find a few others around the world, but not many. They theorized—because doctors need labels for everything—that kids like Austin had most likely been erroneously diagnosed as autistic and treated as such, which was why there was so little authentic documentation available.

Even when I was old enough to understand that my big brother was "different," he'd never spoken a single word and hated being touched. He'd mostly accepted Mom bathing him without having a screaming fit, but if he did start screaming, it scared the hell out of me. He'd make this screeching sound, like somebody strangling a bird, and my heart would just about explode with fear. Fortunately, those mega fits didn't happen often.

Whatever it was that made Austin "different," my parents had to adopt methods and skills for taking care of him. So did I, but those "skills" didn't help against jerkwads at school who called my brother a retard.

Yeah, I admit it, Austin embarrassed me. Other guys talked about how badass their big brothers were, and mine was "different." I didn't understand why he was different, but I did know those kids were dissing my family, so what was I supposed to do except punch 'em out? That's how I got a rep early on for being a "troubled kid." Since when did standing up for your brother make you troubled?

Once, when he was pulling me off a kid I'd been fighting, the principal told me I'd come to a bad end if I didn't change. "Learn to control your temper, Colton."

Did I have friends in those early grades? Yes and no. After some kids got used to Austin being around, they'd come over for birthdays and play dates. We always had a blast, especially in the pool during the summer. But as I moved up in grades, I got into more fights because of kids using the "R" word about Austin. Suddenly, even my friends' parents didn't want me at their homes, and they always seemed to have "something planned" when Mom invited their kids to hang with me.

Defending my brother turned me into an angry, lonely kid. Sure, I could've laughed every time someone used the "R" word, and I even did a few times. But later, I'd feel guilty for letting the kid diss my brother and I'd punch him out anyway. I got called "Psycho Boy" by one kid I beat up in the fourth grade and that name stuck to me like gum.

* * *

I have to admit that, despite all my anger, Austin still intrigued me. He could look at something that was backwards and figure out what it was, even complex words he didn't know the meaning of. He also loved looking into mirrors - not at himself, but at the room behind him, so my parents installed mirrors all over the house because those mirrors calmed him. He even watched TV reflected in a mirror—mostly science shows, which I thought was strange. Most of the time, when we were together, he'd stare at my reflection, rather than directly at me, which I found pretty creepy. Like I said, Austin was different.

His biggest obsessions, hands down, were rain and rainbows. He *lived* for rainy days. He'd stand at the window of his upstairs room and watch the raindrops fall, his expression immobile as a rock.

At first, Mom tried to draw him away from the window and get him to play with a toy or color something. "C'mon, sweetie, you've been watching the rain for hours. Aren't you bored yet?"

She would gently nudge him, but he always shook her hand loose and continued staring at the rain as though it held all of life's secrets. When mom made the mistake of trying to force him, the choking-bird screech erupted, and my heart would start pounding. I'd run into the room to find Austin with his fists clenched, looking at mom and screaming bloody murder.

The first time this happened I was only four years old, but I still remember saying to her, "He likes the rain, mommy."

I'd seen him do the staring thing before and, young as I was, I understood that this was Austin's "thing." Rain. In truth, I *thought* it was the rain until I was seven and he was ten. That's when I realized it was the *rainbow* he waited for. When that realization struck me one day, I put aside my video game console and entered his room. I'd heard the rain letting up and wondered what he would do when it stopped.

He stood by his window as usual. Then he did something I'd never seen before—he turned to me and pointed outside. I don't think Austin had ever looked straight at me before (like I said, he usually looked at my reflection in a mirror.)

I walked past his bed and stood beside him. Outside, the rain had become light showers, and a rainbow had appeared in the distance. It stretched across the sky and seemed to touch down right smack in the woods blanketing Mount Tam.

And that's what Austin pointed at.

"You like rainbows, don't you, Austin?"

Of course, he didn't answer me. He lowered his arm and strode to his drawing table, shoved a pile of blocks onto the carpet and pulled out some blank paper. Then he sat on the floor, legs folded under him and began to draw. Curious, I eased nearer to watch. With Austin you never knew if sudden movements might set him off. I slid his desk chair over and sat beside him.

What had always seemed weird to me was the direction Austin drew. He was right-handed, like me, but I either started in the center of the paper or tended to draw like I wrote, from left to right. Austin began on the right side of his paper and drew from right to left. At first, I was tempted to try and correct him, but after teachers gave up having him write his name because he always wrote it backwards, I ignored his unusual method. Like I said before, "backwards" was kind of his thing all around.

Within twenty minutes, he'd created an amazing likeness of the mountain forest outside his window. The rainbow looked so realistic I reached out to touch it. Austin set aside his colored pencils and sat back, staring at the image as though mesmerized. Then he looked at me. *Straight* at me. He was trying to tell me something. I didn't understand it then, not until years later, but he *was* trying to communicate.

I was only seven. What was I supposed to do? I just said, "Super cool picture, Austin."

He stared a moment longer, as though seeing right through me. Then he looked back out the window, and I followed his gaze. The rainbow had vanished. I turned back and almost gasped. For the first time in my life, Austin's face displayed a trace of emotion—sadness.

That was the first of a hundred rainbow drawings my brother crafted, each more photo realistic than the previous. He had the gift all right. He also liked to free-hand draw some of my comic book covers, especially *Reverse Flash* or *Bizarro Superman* comics (which were his favorites), and he reproduced them with stunning perfection. Both comics involved reverse versions of the superheroes.

Occasionally, when he stood at the window staring out at the woods, I'd join him, hoping I might see what he saw. Sometimes at twilight, I'd see movement among the trees, like shadows shifting places. It was probably caused by the setting sun, but I imagined monsters roaming around out there and felt a little freaked out.

But Austin would stand at the window till well after dark as though he was listening for something. I never heard a sound, and I don't think he did, either. On rainbow days, I'd see him tilting his head slightly from side to side. He'd keep his body rigid and his gaze riveted on whatever he saw out there, but I never spotted anything except the rainbow above the forest.

My parents did everything they could for him. My mom tried to bond with Austin by coloring with him. But the moment she praised him with even a slight pat on the back, he recoiled like she was a snake. I saw how much that hurt her. True, she's the only person Austin allowed to dress him and help him with bathing and other personal stuff.

But he never hugged her, and even back then I saw how much she needed him to love her. Now, after everything that's happened, I know he *did* love her. He just wasn't able to show it. But I'm getting ahead of myself. I better get to that horrible day when Austin disappeared.

It was the only time my mother ever hit me.

www.ingramcontent.com/pod-product-compliance
Lightning Source LLC
LaVergne TN
LVHW091633070526
838199LV00044B/1049